I0600654

All Rights Reserved.

Copyright © 2026 Juan J Alemán II

No part of this publication may be
reproduced, distributed, or transmitted in any
form or by any means, including
photocopying, recording, or other electronic
or mechanical methods, without the prior
written permission of the publisher, except as
permitted by U.S. copyright law. For
permission requests, contact Juan Alemán II.

ISBN: 979-8-9996710-6-6 Paperback

ISBN: 979-8-9996710-5-9 Hardcover

ISBN: 979-8-9996710-7-3 EPub

The story, all names, characters, and incidents
portrayed in this production are fictitious. No
identification with actual persons (living or
deceased), places, buildings, and products is
intended or should be inferred.

Book Cover Art by Alicia Arbaszewski
Section Illustrations by Juan Alemán II,
Via Co-pilot AI
Edited By: Sean Leonard
Published By:
All Words Are for My Mental Health
First Edition 2026

Meanderings & Melancholy:

Poetry, Essays, and Stories

By:

Juan J Alemán II

"The ability to understand is closely linked to wanting to know the truth."

Table of Contents

~ Poetry ~

Table of Contents

~ Essays ~

Table of Contents

~ Stories ~

And some bonus material.

Foreword:

Weaving a story is sometimes easy, but it is sometimes a scary and humbling experience. When I started writing the material in this collection, I was afraid that my characters didn't have a story to tell. But they continued to speak to me. So, the following is what they shared.

With all the blemishes, stretch marks, and bad breath of a waking adult. Skimming somewhere between the ether of imagination and the halls of reality. As unpredictable as I feel many days, I have come to love the ability to find escape from time to time.

Many of the things in my imagination might seem dark at times, but there is hope at the end of the pages. The moments spent between the beginning and the end are our special moments to share from here to the end of time.

Thank you for sharing some time with me. *"The invisibility of sadness should not stop us from sharing a smile with others."*

--Juan J Alemán II, Puyallup, WA, 2025

I wish to dedicate this book to:

Any family who lost a service member to conflict somewhere in the world without a goodbye or who lost a veteran that found their way home from combat only to lose the battles that followed them home—my heart breaks for each of you.

And with love,

Beth, Damian, & Margaret for being there even when I didn't deserve your love, understanding, and confidence.

Poetry

"I scream with fear into the abyss — It screams back in anger."

Decisions and Truth

The idea that we have free will is fleeting

We answer every day not only for our own decisions, but for the decisions of others.

It's all interconnected.

Hate from someone three degrees from us will trickle down

Then the anger comes home…

It starts there and becomes ever more difficult to manage

The only truth is that our reactions make us.

Our truth is the willingness to say,

"You do not make my choices."

"I choose what I am."

"Only I control me."

Lies and Promises

The promise is that I'll love you forever,

The lie is that I'll love you forever.

The promise is that I'll tell always you the truth,

The lie is that I'll always tell you the truth.

The promise is that I'd give my life for you,

The lie is that I'd give my life for you.

The contradictions in life are often first given to us when

We are children…

Be nice to people that need it,

Treat all people with respect,

Honesty is the best policy.

The lies and promises in life are both lessons and

punishments.

Happiness

I try to find the words, but they elude me.

The difficulty is that there is none in my heart.

No pain or sorrow, just none of it.

No future, no past in it.

I stare at the endlessness of possibilities and know that there

will never be one moment of... happiness.

Snow

I walk into the snowy night; my hands dig deeply into my pockets and search for warmth that they will not find. On these snowy nights, the walks into the infinity of white blankets make me feel free. I'm not walking away; it's more like a break in my mind.

Everything was so cut and dry when she said that it was over. The cut makes it seem like it just happened, but it's been months.

Sarah had found walking away from the life that we made look easy. I still think of her, seeing her walking down the hallways of the house that we had turned into a home. So, I walk.

Luckily, we'd never had children. No pets. The custody of our joint friends had gone to Sarah. But she was so ready to leave that I got to keep the house. Who she is with, where she might be, or even what she is doing now, I don't know. What I do know is that my snowy walks grow longer each day.

Peace, I've discovered, is hard to find when you feel alone. Interestingly, loneliness is not much of a motivator to do much of anything with your life. So, I walk day in and day out.

What am I walking to? Why does it even matter

without Sarah?

These are the questions that fly through my mind as I walk into the snowy nights. The snow has become a buffer between the rest of the world and me. It has changed my image of the meaning of snowed in.

I could leave at any time; I could jump in my car and go into town. Have a beer at the local pub with a crowd of people that don't know Sarah and don't know me. I could pick a date for the night. Show my prowess as a man and get her a cab the next morning while I have my morning coffee.

But I'm mentally snowed in, my car is stuck. My mind is just as stuck as a snow-blind hunter.

I'm going nowhere today, and it doesn't appear that I will leave this place anytime soon. When you are snowed in, the outside world may as well be a million miles away.

So, I walk farther from the house; the warmth and shelter are there, but I just don't feel like I deserve the comfort. Was it all my failure? People that deserve to be left are left behind. So, Sarah leaving was my fault, right? But what did I do wrong?

I walk and replay every moment; the good, the bad,

the happy, and the angry. I just need to find the moment where it all fell apart. Where everything simply fell apart. Why did Sarah walk through that door, get into her car, and never look back at me.

I know, I watched her the entire time. She never looked back.

I should turn back toward the house. I'm far too cold to continue walking away, but I'm not turning around. I don't deserve the comfort or warmth. It's a funny thing, but even tears come out cold after walking in the freezing weather long enough. Infinity is not too far when you are going nowhere.

Missing You

There's an ache in my brain

I can't stop it from thinking of you.

The burning in my chest is the sting of my heart's tears…

I am missing you…

People will say that the feelings of sadness go away.

That there is a lifetime yet to live.

Why stay in this moment?

Why?

We were tied together from the moment I knew you.

From the first words we shared.

To the last breaths we shared.

The laughs. The tears. The anger. The love.

You are gone, but all that will not be gone until we are joined again.

Until that moment, I'll miss you.

The Warrior Does Not Die Alone

He enters the barracks, the smell is fear, sweat, pain cream, and tears. The next eight weeks will turn these men into brothers. But like all relationships, nothing will be easy.

The days and nights begin to roll into one another. This culture that we create scares many. We yell about killing and making the grass grow with blood. We fight one another to see which man will stand in there and take the hits.

It's not always the strongest that stay standing, it's will and smarts that often make the leaders out of the outliers.

One thing to know is that you don't look back.

You don't wait for trouble. You take perfect 30" steps, your body is 40" all around.

The longer we are together, the more hate there is between some of us, but you can't hate what you don't love. We grow unruly, on weekend passes we become belligerent with alcohol and visit the lingerie shops to get samples of the goods.

We walk a stage, our families watch, but we have our

eyes on one another. For we are no longer recruits; we
few have become soldiers. We soldiers are now warriors
for life. As we part, we part as warriors.

We may never meet again in this world, but we will
meet again.

Years have passed and I'm on patrol. The enemy never sleeps,
neither do we. We walk the dark nights into the darkest hours.
We keep our eyes peeled and our minds aware. There are not
winners in war… This I know as I settle to rest.

No, there are only survivors. But for every brother lost on
foreign soil, they live on in the memory of their fellow
warriors. The day passes, I think of home. The night passes, I
dream of death.

I will be 21 next week. In the States, I'm old enough to
vote, here I'm old enough to kill, but in the States, I will
never have the opportunity to buy a beer.

It was a Thursday; I followed the same steps that I did
every day before beginning patrol. The new guy never
felt the pressure from the landmine. I heard it for an
instant, but if you hear it, you're too fucking close to do
anything about it.

I feel the heat and pressure. I can't hear anything.
I'm fighting for air, and the pressure feels like it crushed my
lungs. I see others weeping, I think I'm doing the same. But it
could be blood instead of tears warming my face. Everyone's

mouths are open, but with no hearing it just looks like a lot of yawning. It struck me as funny for a moment. We're all so tired that we are going to die of boredom.

I lay near the new kid; it's just his top half and I'm just holding onto the bit of his forearm left below his right elbow. The long beep in my ear is annoying and makes it hard to think. I squeeze his arm and give him a glance and I manage to smile. I can't hear him, but I do know that he is crying. I don't have words because my lungs have no air. It grows dim and I remember that Orson Welles once said something about us "being born and dying alone."

Sure, I was born alone. No breathing, well, that can't last forever, and for me it was just over a minute. But I'm a member of a group of warriors worldwide that know one thing… A warrior does not die alone.

The To-Do List

To my son.

You arrive today; we must get to the hospital soon.

Your room is ready, diapers aplenty.

The house has been made as a secure fortress just
for your safety.

I painted your room; you're a Pooh guy.

You're a year old today, the party is far too big, and you
won't remember it.

It's part of the list to video, picture, and capture
each moment, should you ever ask.

You're two years old; your sister has arrived.
We hope you will be forever friends.

You smile; you want to hold her. You want to be a good
big brother.

You're four years old, we must enroll you
in a reasonable pre-school.

We hear of your days, we hear of your friends, you've
started the part of the journey where you will do your own
things.

It's summer, you're playing football. You don't like it…
Not at first.

I tell you, just finish the season. I tell you this every day.

It will be a while, but you love playing. You
love competing.

You're a teenager, we lost you somewhere along
the way.

It hurts to see it, but we are on opposite sides of the world.

I cry. I cope. I self-medicate. I know where you saw it now.
You're seventeen, you finished school!

We shared a cry; we were finding each other
through the fog.

You're twenty-one, you're becoming the man I knew that
you could be.

I must be here to continue to help.

I must teach you the things that you must do.

But the best laid plans…

I won't be here, not forever, I won't see the
finished product.

So, do this with your time: Find your own

path.

Stand for what you know is right.

Visualize your success.

And if you ever feel like you've finished… Look to the horizon, I'll give you an idea.

Thoughtful or Thoughtless

Are my thoughts thoughtful or thoughtless?
Are the words I use necessary or just mean?
Do I always need the last word?
I look into the mirror of my life's choices and,
yes, I've been incessantly mean and petty.
The hardest thing to see in life is the wrong that we do.
The sadness that we spread.
Anger is typically the fuel. Attitude is the ride.
Open your eyes and imagine, you're full of attitude…

And you're angry again, what better thing to do
than make the others around us regret their being
there.
Every day, we face challenges.
What will I wear?
Should I say that?
What did they do to deserve that?
They all did something…
I should fear nothing, right?
Their feelings are nothing to me…
I guess I am just thoughtless.

Delusions

Grandeur and grace give us a bloated feeling of
self-worth.
Are we victims of circumstance, or do we create
the circumstances that plague us?
If our lives were books, are we page turners
or pretenders?
Be grateful for the moments that we have with the ones
that we love…
Creating memories, making the most of summer
days and fall nights.

The young never know the gift of the future is nothing to
be taken for granted, the young walk a path that is still
long. That is full of potential love, strife, and everything
else that comes in between.

Five decades of life…

Over fifty years, and there is no rhyme or reason for what
happens. All the ones that raise you must go, first,

And next, friends, associates, and colleagues will take
that long road. The real delusion?

Is to believe that we won't join them.

Visions of Grandeur

My life is much more than my ideas of what I want…

I am what I make of myself. I am what I aspire
to become. I am…

The moments I spend looking to others are wasted. No
one can help me, but me.
My safe place is my mind. There I become who I was
meant to be…
I've heard that delusions make you unable to attain better
status.
I call bullshit on that. As I sit in my apartment and stare
at MY walls.

I look at and read my plans. I know where I am going.
I know…

Into the Eyes of My Love

I saw her, I almost walked by, but there was that moment
that we locked eyes.

She was younger than me, too pretty for me, and not a
match for me in any way; yet she looked at me in a way
that I had looked at her.

You never forget.

You never know when you have met the person that you will
spend your life with.

Until they become the person that you

spend the rest of your life with.

Movie love would have you believe you'll trip or fall
when your eyes lock.

That's a myth. You stop.

Your body stops, in that moment, to capture
every smell, sound, and moment.

You've found it.

Love.

It's interesting, the feeling in your stomach the first time that you say it to that person, and they say it back to you.

I've never thought that there is just one person, a soulmate if you will, for anyone.

I think of loving someone as feeling affection without it being work.

Real love is never work.

Relationships, they're a different beast, but let's focus on love.

For almost thirty years, I have stared into the eyes of my love.

We have stared into each other's eyes… Into the eyes of our children.

Maybe, just maybe, into the eyes of our grandchildren.

A life spent with someone that you love is priceless.

The moments wane on into the night and we blink into sleep, but for just a bit longer I stare into the eyes of my love.

For Just a Moment

For my daughter

For just a moment, I held you and comforted you
till you slept.

For just a moment, I held your hand while you learned to
skate.

For just a moment, I watched you get onto a school bus.

For just a moment, you were learning to play
the violin…

Learning to paint…

Learning to be who you would become.

Your love for life, your smile, and your never-flinching
enthusiasm have always been a credit to you.

As my moments wane in this world, I will still watch
your moments continue.

We exist for all the happiness, sadness, and
moments that make our memories.

One day my moments will end, and for just a moment, I
will leave you and you will miss me.

But know that each moment I shared with you, each

moment that you watched me, and each moment that became our memories are there for you when you need.

For just a moment, we live this existence.

The one life that we receive, the one family we raise, the ones that earn our love.

Those people make all the moments worthwhile.

I love you.

I Guess it's Just Me

The moments wane away as I stare into nothing and wish
for something, anything, to change. A chance to be better
Tomorrow than I felt today.

Still, I cry.

I can't control my mind; so how am I supposed
to Control the world around me: How I react
to what I fear,
to what follows me and makes me stare over
my shoulder.

Every waking hour, it all floods into my brain again.
I'm alone. There are no prizes around the corner,
no family to call, no friends to lean on.

I stare at this cell phone; it could have been a lifeline.

Instead, it only reminds me of those that are no
longer there.

Those that never reached out to me.

Those that moved forward and never really needed me.
There is a small smirk as the tears warm my cheeks,
the smirk, does it fool me?

But it does hide my utter pain. My mind feels as if it's
melting.

Every moment of every day, I draw closer to my
end and, subsequently,

"Who will mourn me?" "Will anyone
weep for me?"

But in this life, we are born alone and… You know the
rest, right?

Or, well, I guess it's just me.

Memories of Sleep

I woke up in a sweat, did I piss during a nightmare, again?

Night after night, it's the same thing…

Meds to find sleep, try to count sheep.

1, 2, 3…

I do not find the rest I seek.

The sandman, bastard that he is, merely laughs as I cry.

The moments continue to drift by.

Sleep, at last I fall down the rabbit hole.

I have deep regrets, sadness, and anger for the things I've done.

Killer, they call me a killer…

Die, it's the point where I sit now.

There must be a reason I made it home.

A reason I can walk, see, hear, and exist.

A reason my friends cannot do any of those things…

It wasn't supposed to be this way; we were supposed to be together.

Recruits on day one, soldiers at the end.

I still see them beside me. Road marching, laughing, and alive.

We shoot, move, and communicate.

The thing is, I sit alone… They didn't come home. I need to find a safe space.

I cry; I want to be with my squad again. We were supposed to be together.

Sole survivor, huh? To me, it's just the last to die.

Walking down the corridors, barracks rooms, and old platoons.

Days gone by… My nights are filled with those days gone by.

Waking in tears, awakened full of fears night in and night out.

I don't wish to die. But I can not find a way to live with my thoughts.

The memories. The moments.

I don't drink it away anymore; my therapist says to use a toolbox.

We add tools to it every appointment.

The only tool I haven't been able to grasp is sleeping without remembering it all.

I feel foolish sitting beside the bed and crying.

Soaked. Sad. Alone.

Alive. Regretful. Alone.

And there's no tool for that.

How does this end? I get to go and meet my friends.

The Worth

The rich man's son, sleeps at home

The poor man's son dies in a different land all alone.

But who cares?

Do money and an excuse, after excuse make it fair?

I've spent a lifetime trying to understand,

What is the exact worth of a man?

Do connections, family, and class automatically make you

better?

And why? Because no one would ever want to help a debtor.

Green is what matters.

And not the OD Green that was given to us on a platter.

Sent away never a chance to say goodbye.

The rich boys will later run the world and the gave them when

we died.

What is the worth of a man?

You might know, if you were willing to go to battle and take a

stand.

Essays

"Anger smothers me like a cruel burlap weighted blanket—the more I push away the heavier it feels"

You're Chicano?

The thing about being Chicano is that you live in a Purgatory, of sorts. You don't belong in Mexico, a lot of Chicanos don't speak Spanish, but in the United States you're called a wetback, beaner, or any other negative name that Americans can come up with. So, again, Purgatory. I was born in South Texas, but after my parents divorced, we moved to a small town in East Texas; it was 99.99% black and white. Then there was my family, the .01%.

It wasn't bad there, but I didn't know anything else. When you become older and then leave as an adult, you see that some things there weren't as good as you thought. True, life being as it is, you understand some of it, but you pretend that you don't get it. Other things go over your head 'cause your called things as a kid. Those are the things that you look back on as an adult and think to yourself,

"What the hell, really? They said that to a kid?"

As an adult, I found out about Brown Pride, being Latino, and what a Chicano really is. All of the things that I never knew because I wasn't in a world to be surrounded by that. I was growing up trying to sound, dress, and talk like everyone around me. And none of that was Latino. When I visited my dad, my cousins thought that my East Texas accent was funny, and the little Spanish I spoke was terrible. So, you withdraw rather than reach out. You don't try to speak any Spanish to them or anyone else after that.

Then, at home, people know you're different. I'm not too dark, but the dark hair was a dead giveaway. So, they ask. I say I'm Mexican. So, now they know, and, of course, I must speak Spanish. Here's a tip: I started learning English at about four or five years old. I pushed myself to learn and be proficient at doing that, so at the time my Spanish

vocabulary was (at best) that of a four-or five-year-

old. Many Chicanos are in the same boat. They start

speaking English at a young age, and although your

parents speak Spanish to you, you respond in

English.

With that being said, my crappy Spanish got me

through high school, but I needed more. More

knowledge and comfort with my native language. It's

a strange feeling to try to communicate with others

when you don't understand or have never heard the

slang being used. I think of all the dialects and slang

words that I know in English. There are that many, if

not more, in Spanish. So I look like a goof trying to

be cool in Spanish. But it comes with the territory.

You may ask why I didn't try harder to be

better at speaking Spanish. It's simple, I didn't want

the thick accent that comes with constantly speaking a different language.

Sure, I had an East Texas accent, but I worked extremely hard to get rid of it after high school. In college, I took speech and diction, learned phonetics, and took a class in stage accents.

Long story short, I have no twang from my early days, but that didn't solve my problem. I'm a Chicano that is terrible at Spanish and knowing my history. And that really sucks. That's the thing that people that know their family's stories and have worked hard to relate to that history have defeated. In college I wrote a paper about how the Latino population was the fastest growing group in the United States, and that is still happening.

In 2022, the GDP (Gross Domestic Product) of U.S. Latinos was $3.7 trillion, which makes it the fifth largest economy in the world. That outpaced India, France, and the United Kingdom. Okay, that's nothing to sneeze at.Latinos are making it happen in the economic world. But the thing that Latinos still do is judge one another for not being Latino enough. It's sad. We can't continue to do that to one another. It's hurtful for those, like me, that don't speak up for themselves. And those that do speak end up in fights with other Latinos. We need more understanding amongst one another and less laughing, pointing, and judging.

So, now on to the show, the reason that I am writing this. It's not to whine, which I know that I have been, a bit, but I feel some way about this. There is a stigma about being macho and not saying, "This is how I honestly feel," when you want to complain about what your life has been.

"It could be worse!" I can hear those around me saying. Or "Be thankful for what you got."

Well, I am very thankful for the life that I lived. I have done a great many things that I am surprised by and proud that I was able to do.
But there is something missing. There are things left to be said. I want to do some sharing, and maybe we can learn from one another along the way. It's simple; life is all about learning. What we are, where we come from, and best of all, where

My grandmother, before she passed away, told me that the only thing that people can never take away from you is your knowledge. She'd been through a lot; an early loss of her parents, being raised by siblings, having nothing, and making a better life for her family and grandchildren. She saved every penny that she could, she and my grandfather worked as caretakers in a secluded place near a lake in East Texas. As kids, we called it the "Big House"—to us, it was the biggest house that we had ever seen. My grandmother told us stories in Spanish; she never pushed us to learn to speak Spanish. That was something that she understood.

There are different ways that people will judge by looks, clothes, or actions—but don't give them any

excuse to judge you further. In speaking with one of my therapists who had a thick German accent, I asked her, "Do people ever judge you because of your accent?"

She thought for a moment, then answered me. "Yes. When a person hears you speak in the United States, and you have any type of accent, they assume that you are not intelligent."

"I know," I replied. "I do find that if you have

any type of accent, you are judged harshly. Two assumptions are made: you aren't from *here* and, since you don't speak English perfectly, there is some type of intelligence reason for it."

I liked her. She was honest and easy to talk to during our sessions. It was nice that she seemed to understand me. Many times, in getting matched with doctors, you don't find someone that you can relate to. But this one worked out. We did speak about my childhood and how I did not feel that I fit in anywhere. Not in South Texas, Mexico, or East Texas. The saddest thing was, I didn't know much else about life.

I want to get into this a bit deeper. Let's discuss Brown Pride, being Latino, and Chicano.

To begin, Brown Pride started as a movement in the 1960s. It was a play on the phrase "Black is

Beautiful" used by African Americans in the 60s. It never had any racist overtones. It was about being proud of where you come from, the color of one's skin, and a voice saying that we will no longer assimilate. Being brown and

Mexican is what I am. As an individual born shortly after that, but a world away, I couldn't relate when I was younger. I was not self-aware. There was so much information about being black and proud. And whether white Americans will admit it or not, American history is told mostly about white people being the saviors of everything around them: freed the slaves, defeated the Mexicans at the Alamo, settled our country. Yes, all done by white America— and then they say, you're welcome!

But Latinos in America have most often been treated as second-class citizens. Being told, "Go back home!" The thing is, my parents were born here, so surprisingly, I am home. Many Chicanos are still afraid to express themselves in public (now more than ever) because they get asked for a green card, a birth certificate, or naturalization papers.

America has made it our burden of proof to not just say, "But I was born here." Now, it's all about pulling over a group of brown people because we can't possibly be from here.

Understand that in 2022, immigrants born in Mexico were just under 11 million people. To put that in context, that was 23% of all immigrants. The largest population of immigrants, at 28%, were from Asia. But we as Latinos are most often told to go back home. All immigrants, unfortunately, do suffer some indignities, and that is sad. But who is anyone to tell someone to leave? I won't start the whole,

"America, love it or leave it." Maybe another time.

But back to my point, you hear more about Latinos being targeted for just existing in the States than any other culture. Yet, the 60s and 70s were all about Brown Pride. In the 80s and 90s, Latinos continued to grow in the United States as a culture and a people. Now, a Latino has to be careful even going to work or to the grocery store, potentially being stopped because "they look like they may be illegal."

What is being Latino? You see, people say "Hispanic" as if that is a people. Well, let's put on our thinking caps, it's time to go to school.

Hispanic is a Latin term that originated in the 16th century. It comes from the word *Hispanicus,* which in turn means "of the Iberian Peninsula." So, it became a thing in the United States government. It started being used by the U.S. Census Bureau in 1980 to describe "people of Spanish origins." This was brought about by the Mexican American Legal Defense Education Fund (MALDEF) and other organizations lobbying the federal government to have our community represented as a distinct ethnic category. Up until that point, Latinos were simply counted as white. Which lumps together people from Mexico, Puerto Rico, Guatemala and Spain. And as we become ever more advanced, the Cen Bureau now has "Another Hispanic, Latino, or Spanish origin." Redundant, right?

But by the 1990s, complaints began at the use of the term. It goes into colonizers and the colonized and how not all Latinos come from Spain. It is a very divided community. Trust me, I was not aware of my apparent dislike for Puerto Ricans until some of my more Mexican friends informed me that it was my duty. The argument, should you wonder, is that Puerto Ricans think that they're special because they are citizens and Mexicans aren't always born as citizens. The end.

Well, I digress… Latino is a term which is a shortening of the word *Latinoamericano*, or "Latin American." This was coined in the 19th century to describe former Spanish colonies.

Those colonies were South America and the Caribbean. Once the colonizers were gone, it became Latin America or the land of Latinos. Ta-da. I'm definitely coining the phrase "land of Latinos." I don't really know what for just yet, but it's mine.

So, I'm not Hispanic. In my opinion, that was just made up by the government to lump brown people together. It is a source of disrespect; you all look alike, and you will be called by the name we give you. The way people see you and what they call you equals the respect that they have for you.

In truth, I'm not Mexican either. I was born in the United States, as were my parents, and my grandmothers. My grandfathers, on the other hand, were born in Mexico. They performed a civic duty by fighting for their adopted country World War II. One staying stateside and one sent to Italy (where the Latinos had their own Unit) Earning citizenship for volunteering to protect this country. Their new home! Others just had money and came over and never had to do anything to earn it. But hey, I'm just saying.

Now, what is a Chicano? The term has a long history, but the first time it is believed to have been used in print is 1911. It was used in the Spanish language newspaper *La Crónica*. Early on, it is believed to have been used as a derogatory term used by more affluent Mexican Americans to describe Mexican Americans of lower social standing—likely with some very intended racial overtones. But, in general, a Chicano is a person of Mexican descent born in the United States.

We move to the 60s and 70s, where Mexican Americans began to take the word back. So much of Latino culture and the culture people of all colors found themselves in was a struggle to find a positive identity. So, being Chicano became a source of pride. It was time to identify a way to take back a word that was never meant to be a negative. It was meant to identify Mexican people born in the United States. But with every positive, there will always be people that want to make it negative for others.

It's those same people that want to judge others

for the life they choose to live. So, not all Chicanos know their past and make friends with more people of other races or other Chicanos that aren't culturally adept. What happens? Welcome to the word *pocho*. Exactly, a Chicano that assimilated into American culture. There are other, much more, rude names. The point is, no matter where you go in life, there will be people that want to judge you for just being you. When I was raising my children, they learned English first, I wanted them to have a command of this language and then learn a second language. Unfortunately, two things ended up happening. First, we never got around to learning too much Spanish. And second, it's my fault. Sure, my Spanish (as w know) wasn't the best, but they have none. In high school, daughter chose French, and she is good. My son is now learning Spanish from an app. Yeah, an app. But I stalled because I wanted them to have a mastery of the language, no hint of an accent that could close any doors for them. It is my fault.

I read an article about Bolivian bombshell, Raquel Welch. Her birth name was Jo Raquel Tejado. Her mother was Anglo and her father refused to speak Spanish to his children in the home. Why? He did not want them to have an accent. I didn't originate it, but I still regret not teaching them. Would people have spent more money to see Rachel Welch or Debbie Welch (both names suggested for her)? No one knows, but she made her mark on the world. You know what? I am Chicano. No matter what anyone says about you, be who you are.

Unabashedly, continue to be you! Will teasing or rude behavior ever end? No. But find the people that make you feel good about being you. Surround yourself with them. *Orale*!

He's the One in Green

I had just finished Basic Training and AIT. I was in Artillery at Fort Sill and we were in the OSUT (One Station Unit Training) program. My family came from Texas to see me graduate. They had always been very supportive, and they all came to be there for me. I was told later by my mother that when she first got there, and we were all marching in by platoon, she was looking around and someone walked up to her and asked if they could help.

"I'm looking for my son," she replied.

The man, being helpful, then asked, "What's his unit and name?"

My mother, in classic mother-style and in a bit of a panic that I would think they had not arrived, responded, "He's the one in the green."

The man chuckled and said, "Let's see if we can

find him."

Of course, they found me, I graduated, and we spent an afternoon together. It was all fun, and we were together all weekend celebrating.

The last part is not true. It was fun, but I told my family that I was going to celebrate the weekend with my friends. They left that afternoon. I was alone. Yes, I partied that night and I forgot a lot of it, but I look back and wish that I had spent that time with my family. Wishes are worth as much as yesterday's lotto ticket that has today's winning numbers. Nothing.

Over the next five years, I had ups and downs. I stayed stateside and safe, but between training and field visits, I started drinking much more than I needed. I drowned the person that existed before I had joined the military.

Between drinks, I found a wife and got out of the Army, but I was searching for peace. A peace that couldn't be found from drinking. But an alcoholic keeps looking in the same place for it every night. Alcoholism is literal insanity: doing the same thing over and over and expecting a different outcome.

I've been married for almost 29 years, my children are adults, and I have been sober for three and a half years. In the time since finishing Basic Training, my world has changed tremendously. My mother passed away in 2009, and my eldest sister lost a cancer battle at the end of 2022. I, myself, am a cancer survivor.

Choices make us who we are. I chose along the way to do some bad things. Fitting in was not easy. In Artillery, it was all testosterone-driven. Whoever could drink the most, party the hardest, and still show up the next morning and sweat it out while running. Oh yeah, and you did it all over again as you grabbed a 40 oz. from the Shoppette directly after final formation. I was lost in a haze of wanting to be that guy. In doing that, I found myself afoul of the law a couple of times. Yes, I actually used "afoul." Basically, I was popped for drinking and driving. My work ethic, showing up each day, helped me stay ahead of those problems.

I did not drink during the day; I would sweat out everything at PT and then work hard all day in the motor pool or in the field when we were out there training. Never for a moment did I let my apparent alcoholism interfere with performance.

I was functioning. Being referred to ADAPC (the alcohol and drug abuse program on post), I found that I had more problems than I thought. But

I didn't follow through; the continuing support from the therapist was needed, but my Unit couldn't allow the time. That is pointing fingers—maybe I could have done something more on my own time? But what therapist was available in the evenings in the 90's? Left alone, no time during working hours, I just moved on down the road. I stopped for a month or two. Over and over, I stopped for a month or more. The push to get better, from outside of myself, was needed.

I could focus on that, or I could look at the sum of my parts and say, "I did okay."

I kept my marriage together and raised my children. I love acting and writing and did get to act professionally. In 2020, I wrote and released a children's book. What I found is that I love writing, creating worlds that existed only in my mind before they found life on the page. Over the next four years,

I began writing short stories and poetry. I had a manuscript edited and published my first short-story collection.

It was scary to put my words out into the ether that is the public eye. I am not sure how I feel about having my ideas being seen by others. Do all authors and artists feel like this about their creations?

In life, we do not have do-overs. At fifty-three years old, I may be in my last chapter. But I still have stories to tell. And I spend my days writing the stories that I have left. Much of my writing is fiction, but some of my life comes through in my words.

The Army did help me find myself in life. I learned real discipline, brotherhood, and purpose in action. I became a better version of myself, and I learned leadership. I took it with me into a career with the government as a civilian.

I loved my time in the Army, and as it ended, I felt like there were so many wasted opportunities. But I guess I did what I was meant to do while there. Our lives are the sum of our experiences, choices, and actions.

As a service entity, the military as a whole needs to recognize and help soldiers when they need help. Leadership will ignore the problems if you keep producing. That has to stop. As an organization, the military needs to learn that hiding the problem is worse than sending a soldier to get treatment. They'll be gone for a few days, but that's better than a life of struggling on their own.

There is no blame to be given. Leadership did what, at the time, was thought to be best for me. I was a hard worker, a self-starter, and I always did the right things at work. It was what happened later in the evenings. Choices. It's all choices.

I chose to drink far too much every day. I didn't go anywhere where alcohol wasn't served. Blacking out was a nightly occurrence; large portions of each night were like VCR tapes that had been erased. Not knowing what you did, how you acted, how you treated people, in retrospect, is horrifying. In your 20s, though, it's a gas!

Being celebrated for being stupid is such an overwhelming thing. I was arrested twice. Once, it was bad. Pleaded down, but bad. And my work ethic saved me. The second time was just because of my prior record. Nothing happened that time and I went home.

I needed help, all of my actions were screaming that. Those needs, though, did not outweigh the needs of the military; again, sharing for transparency. So, you keep working hard during work hours and your life is acceptable. I'm still here, and no, my choices were not acceptable. The life I was making was going to make what lay ahead difficult for me, for my family. Yeah, it sucks when you make choices that negatively impact the ones you love. That was when things changed.

Stopping all of the alcohol use was not even a conscious choice, it just happened. All of the classes, therapy, and trying; one night you take a drink, and the next day you wake up and you don't drink that day, then the next, and the next. The time just adds up. I'm now a relaxed guy who spends his time with his wife learning to be empty-nesters and who walks his do when he can. No drinking. No erased VCR tape, just actual living. It's different for everyone around me. I don't preach and tell people not to drink. Everyone has to make their own choice in that regard. I do know that for me, it was no longer a thing to do. It's been over four years since I

woke up and didn't take that drink. And it's been well

over thirty years since I was the one in green.

Confessions of a Never Was

It's the fourth quarter, senior year, and it's going to be his last football game. Not just of this season, but of the rest of his life. It happens every year in cities all over the country, guys with dreams of being pros ending their short careers. Sometimes, they become "someone" in their small towns. They feel grandiose, they are big stuff in their own minds.

Then there are the other millions, the ones that don't have the opportunity to become a has-been. You know the guy, still goes to high school parties three and four years after leaving. Three and four decades later, they show up at reunions still thinking those few years really mattered. Here's a hint for those that never had the experience of becoming a has-been: it *does* matter to those guys.

It matters to every guy that wanted those moments. That sat on a bench in any sport and then never had their moment. Through the 70s and 80s, it was all about sports. But as we grow and change, failure comes on all levels, whether it's academics, acting, or other ventures. It seems that the more we advance, the weaker our minds become.

Sure, it sounds like a complaint about our society, but truly, it's not. I think about a tug-of-war match in first grade. Always large (okay, so I was a fat kid!), I loved games where my weight helped me. Red Rover? Forget about it, I broke up

Red Rover lines like Pac-Man ate dots! Generally, this was the gist of it: you did what you were good at doing. If you were fast, you ran. If you were strong, you used your strength and so on. Heavy? Use that. Whatever made you special, it earned ribbons and medals. Then, somewhere along the way…

Okay, you know where I'm going. So don't complain, just listen. Somewhere along the way, our strengths stopped earning those awards. Somewhere down the line, someone decided that everyone earns, not just a ribbon, but a trophy. That's right! In the beginning, everyone earned different color ribbons.

Everyone over forty knows what place you earned from the color of the ribbon. Blue, first place. Red, second place. And third place? White! Of course, some places continued with the ribbons up until sixth place, but really, after third place, who cared?

But now, show up in uniform and hang out for the season and, like magic, you get a trophy. Why? What was accomplished over this glorious season?

No scores were kept. No one is a special athlete; you know, the kind to keep an eye on in the future. Sure, there are some tournaments and select teams that do compete. Many of them will be of the has-been crowd. But our trophy collectors? They are going to be of the never was group.

Is it mean or just observant? The one who's affected by that will claim it to be mean; it's old thinking. People from the 1900s thought that way, we're more advanced now—it's a kinder, gentler society, and maybe I just don't belong in that polite society. Then again, our society may be on the edge of total decay. The way we have started to coddle our younger generation is a bit of an over-correction. Let's think of it as a driver that fell asleep at the wheel. They wake up in the wrong lane. What happens next? Well, in an ideal situation, they would end up back in the proper lane and make it home safely. But in the case of a generation that can't accept that not everyone is going to play the game by their rules, what happened is we over-corrected and hit a tree on the opposite side of the road.

So, grandparents stare at the progeny of their children, and they see people that they love, but not necessarily people that they like. It's a difficult and painful concept. It goes back to the old phrase that you can't choose your family. You get what you get.

Clarity being what it is in hindsight, how many of today's parents might have changed what they did? 1922 is recognized as the first-time participation trophies were assigned (I can't say that they were earned), and it didn't just become the standard right away. So, what changed?

People raised by parents that felt that their parents had been too tough changed it all. Kids from the 70s and 80s found themselves remembering difficult times. Mom and Dad having unattainable goals for them. Not winning an award nor even making it up onto the stand when winners were called out. So, they woke up feeling like they were on the wrong side of the road and...yeah, they over-corrected.

Tournaments and games with no scores, no league

champions because "we're all winners," and the worst of parents complaining about grades gets their child a passing grade. Accountability has become a thing of the past. The "no child left behind" generation; well, they became the parents of today. And they would make any excuse to make their own children not be held accountable for learning what they deserve, an unsavory attitude, and no real chances for advancement. And why? Because no one loses in this game.

When the "greatest country" in the world has an entire generation of people thinking that they can be influencers. Yes, they believe goofy videos and dangerous challenges will be entertaining when they are forty. Yes, it's like the forty-year-old guy that shows up at a high school party because it was his alma mater. Cool then is not cool now, but we are where we are. We must admit that there is a definite problem. Teens putting things online that don't belong there. Intimate details are left for all to see. These people, with no discernible talents, are not getting an education. Instead, they make a bit of money and will have no way to maintain this through their lives. So, we are at the end of the first quarter of the twenty-first century, and a majority of this generation is living off of their parents.

That's all we need, parents that will never retire because their children can't hold a real job. And no one thinks that the videos being made by twenty and thirty somethings are not as cute as when they were teenagers.

The generation still has time. But there must be a change, now. The parents must remember how they got to who and what they have by choice. They bought a home, had a couple cars, and lived a life. Now the children of no consequence; well, they will only be as capable as their family built them. With no change, we will fall apart. One who cannot support themselves will not be able to maintain themselves and a family in the future. And now, instead of finding reasonable jobs after college, we have people on the streets asking to get school debt forgiven. Now, why incur the debt if you are choosing to ask to just not pay it? Ex-students have many choices in terms of the degree of their choice.

But, if you chose a degree with no job market, whose fault is that? Or the chosen degree is just not what they thought it was going to be. Is there not sometime, say two years or more, when a student decides, "This may not be for me."

Yet here we are. Protests instead of standing in line at the employment commission.

Amongst the many tough decisions, one has to make in life, college is one of those choices. Not to harp, but why take a loan for an excessive amount of debt on the gamble that your degree will end up garnering you the job of your dreams? Sadly, something else comes to mind.

The loans. In all actuality, the loans are somewhat concerning and predatory. First time at the table for attending college? Have they got a loan for you. Older students going back to school and have terrible credit? Sign right here, Mr./Ms. Student. It's all like some used car salesmen or carnival barker.

"Step right up! We have a loan for you! How about you, sonny? Hey there, pretty lady! We're having a big loan sale today. Buy now, pay later!"

Students sign on the dotted line, and four years or more later when the bill comes in, they want to stand up and say no fair. I didn't get the job I wanted. I didn't finish my degree. Blah, blah, blah...

Well, it's a bit late. Again, it's choices in life that make us who are. Why, then, should one pay for a home loan, auto loan, and other loans; then, student loans fall under some magical category? My mortgage isn't fair; not gonna pay. Nah, doesn't work.

That was sort of a strange blip. Where I don't find it fair that I have to pay for services rendered. I don't want to pay so I'll complain until all my wishes are met?

The phrase "it's not fair" is thrown around a lot these days. Like Jareth told Sarah, "You say that so often, I wonder what your basis for comparison is?" All these former students, unless there is change, will not find a primrose path after their parents are gone.

Still, millennials are getting older day by day, yet they are not getting wiser. The one phrase I took away from Ancient and Medieval Philosophy is, "Experience isn't wisdom, because you can't teach it."

What does it mean? No matter how many times I tell an inexperienced person, "If you touch that fire, it's going to burn you," until they touch the fire and burn themselves, they can't understand what it means or how it feels. So how do you teach or tell someone that you don't always get a trophy, you're not always chosen, or you just aren't that special when, for their entire lives, they've heard all those things about them? They don't win the fake first place that never existed when they have grown up.

So, how does one sum up? Who runs the asylum, when there are only patients?

When did the clowns begin running the circus?

Gen-X painted their children into a corner. Sure, the children need to figure out a creative and logical solution. It's never too late. Change can happen at any time, but the ones that need to change must realize it.

It'll never be easy to look back and tell your children that their failure is your fault, but the longer we think that everything that they do is precious, right, and excusable, the longer they will fail to advance themselves. The sad fact of it all is they were taught to fail.

Yes, we did that.

The Facts of it All

Excuse the subtle diatribe… Maybe we need to be like our grandparents. Is that too much? You hear, almost every day now, that children have no respect. They have no manners or home training. Now, whose fault could that be? The parents? The grandparents? Maybe it's society's fault…

Well, I have an opinion. Thus, the diatribe. But of course, don't we all have our opinions? Whose opinion matters? I have so many questions, but I digress (fun word, huh?). I was going to give some facts. So, away we go.

Growing up in the 70s and 80s, life was quite different. The world was not the sensitive place that we live in now. Sure, there were bullies, guns, people that were LGBTQ, trans individuals. In other words, there is nothing new under the sun in today's world that wasn't there then. I believe the difference is who raised each generation. Parents born in the 40s and

50s grew up after Dr. Benjamin Spock released a book about parenting. Basically, children need structure and schedules, and they have thoughts of their own that need to be nurtured. At the time, this was quite a change in raising children. So, my parents, and the parents that raised their 70s and 80s children, had been raised that way. But then we had another major shift, this being that there was a recession. Then, both parents in the home had to find work. All the structure that Dr. Spock had given our grandparents went out the window.

Sure, there were things to do at school (if you were of age to actually have school activities, and in small towns all over the country, there wasn't a lot for younger kids to do). But in retrospect, kids in general were home alone. Both parents were working, you were alone watching TV and doing your homework till they got home. If you were lucky, someone came home and made dinner. If not, well, you fended for yourself. 80s kids, we made do. You grew up quickly, because you had to do just that.

So, what we had happened was that grandparents were now tasked, during the summers, to watch the children. Our overbearing grandparents, from a completely different time and parenting style, started watching us. We think about how we are treated, how we just want to be home, how our parents must not care if they are leaving us here.

A very natural reaction happens in our minds. "I'll never treat my kids like this!" I believe that this shift made this generation (our kids) more sensitive and not accepting of discipline, rebuke, and feedback. Our children live in a world where discipline is seen as negative. Where corporal punishment is a no-go! A world where every quirk has a diagnosis. Children aren't poorly behaved, ill mannered, or lazy. They have ADHD, ADD, OCD, or any other thing that you can give them.

I personally had bullies in junior high. I dreaded school, and my mother went to school to ask the administration to help me in some way. The principal says he'll do something; she leaves happy. Then what happened next?

"Boy, don't be a pussy! You had your momma come up here for that bullshit? You go out there and take care of your problem, because if you come back here, I'll beat your ass." (That was when teachers and principals could beat you with a wooden board!)

So, I was alone. I was fat, a nerd, and a loner. Sorry to say, but in today's world, that person becomes a threat to others. I didn't let that stop me. I did what that man said, I stood up for myself. It didn't go well at first, but they eventually left me alone. In life, you have to stand up for yourself—if not, you will always, always be fodder for people that prey on the weak.

Honestly, the one thing that never changes is bullies! People of all walks of life and through the remainder of their lives are bullies. Trust me, if someone is an asshole as a kid, teen, or young adult—they will always be an asshole to people that they think they can bully for their entire lives! That is a sad fact of life.

Now, let's continue. I find that everyone has a fascination with being "triggered!" When did that happen? Rather than accepting feedback, truth, or tough love; people will fold up their tents and scream, complain, and whine. When did we become so weak-minded that we can't just accept what other people say as just their opinion? Opinions are a right, you may not agree with mine. That is quite all right, you don't have to accept my thoughts as truth. It won't trigger me. It's a point that should not escape you. Think about that. Someone does something "ableist" (whatever that may be) or anti-"*you fill in the blank*". Then they are cancelled! Cancelled? That's what we used to say about TV shows that didn't make it. Now we describe individuals that say something unpopular (with just about any group!) as cancelled.

There is something so wrong with that. If you disagree... I'm not sorry! I shouldn't be sorry for speaking my mind. I don't have to apologize for having an opinion that YOU don't happen to agree with. What if the words that you are saying, your opinions, or your attitude offend me? I guess that's what it all comes down to. I say something that you don't like, you complain to the Social Media Gods, and *voila*, you cancel me. But I don't agree with you, I'm not cancelling you. I am of the unpopular opinion in life that we all have a right to our own feelings and opinions.

Yes, there is responsibility and weight to our opinions, our deeds, and the words that we choose. At the same time, they're my words and opinions. I do not agree with everyone and I, too, may complain online. But I don't want anyone out of business, or people cancelled. I do feel that opinions are posted and spoken as facts; well, there is that line where many will be trodden by some. Nothing good comes from that, and many people in the world today don't even research what they see online or hear in podcasts. It's just taken as facts.

It really is all so strange, a person reaching out, saying that they are part of an under-represented group. Then, they point their fingers for a short while, until someone more under-represented comes along and points a finger at them for saying something that was offensive to the more of the under-represented person. And the world continues to spin around. My, but ain't the internet a fickle bunch?

I know that this will ruffle feathers, people will think that I am a mean guy for stating my opinions. But, you know, that's okay. I believe that everyone deserves their voice, but why do some feel that their voice is more important than anyone else? Individuals that feel under-represented are the biggest complainers. There is this belief that if you don't have "classic" opinions that you should matter more. The people that feel that they are "different" are the ones wielding their opinions like swords, making others feel as if they can't share their opinion without the world "cancelling" them.

I'm sensitive to others, but I can't stand   the

feeling that some individuals should have more say in

the world. Do parents need to toughen up? Maybe,

but that's up to them. What kind of child do you

want to raise? Take time to think it over. No reason to

rush. If you do not yet have children, think a bit about the

question. Now, if you have children. Take it all in really

deeply. You already have the future generation growing up

in your home. So, again, what type of child do you wish to

raise? Just asking for general purposes…

Again, the responsibility of how a child grows

up is the parent's job. Are they respectful? Do they

say please and thank you? Is the child going to be

able to survive in the world on their own? Will they

be capable of making a home and raising a family of

their own?

Each generation has a way of affecting the next

generation, but it's the choices we make that will

have the effect upon the youth that will eventually be the ones raising children of their own. The ideas that they pass on come from who? Us.

So, the facts… Many of the 70s and 80s kids raised an over-sensitive and, at times, weak-minded generation. We swore that we would not treat our children like our parents treated us. We would be there, we would pay attention, pat them on the back and tell them they are doing everything perfectly! Our children are the "we don't keep score, everybody is a winner, and we all get trophies" generation! The "why do they even compete? Is it a competition? It's just another day in the park" generation.

And finally, the summation of this little essay. Gen-Xer's never wanted to be their parents. In doing that, we created this generation of young men and women. If we aren't happy, who is to blame? Well, look in the mirror. We were the ones that raised them, taught them that they are always right, that everyone is a winner, that adults don't have the right to discipline them, some books deserve to be banned, that teachers and scientists are not experts in their chosen fields and should be ignored at will, that you are number one.

What we did was a disservice to our parents and will be even more to us when we are stepping aside, and they are the adults, the working class, the government...

Will the next *leaders* be ready? Will a society that knows no sense of responsibility or even how to accept criticism be able to lead the world?

As strange as it seems, we will be facing this farce of a new world very soon. Is it too late to change anything? Any little bit of it? No, but we must start speaking plainly to one another. Adults must learn to be responsible for their words, deeds, and choices. We are one people on this Earth, the one Earth that we get, and the one people that we can be. Time for tough love? Time for learning quickly about growing up? Time to speak plainly.

Short Stories

"Tell me a story to make me cry,"
she says. I begin with, "I was born
in 1972…"

The View from the Bottom

We very often look out at others. A world beyond our own that is all around us, always ebbing and flowing, moving at a speed that we can only imagine.

My name is Anton. I'm 16 and a half, and I've been living on the streets of Seattle for about eight months. It's not bad here. I try to stay away from the touristy places—those people don't want to see us. They look the other way because all their money is for their fucking vacation.

I've met a few people since moving here. Matty and Jana are just a year older than me; they ended up on the streets after their parents were killed in a vehicle accident. They were sent to foster care and hated it there… so, *voila*, they ended up here. I was from a small town south of Olympia, Washington. I sold a few things and caught a bus heading north, and I stayed on it as far as my few dollars would take me. Once in the city, everybody finds out what they're made of sooner or later when they find themselves on the street. I guess you might want to know what sent me away from home. It's not pretty story, but an all-too common one in small towns. In big cities, people worry about strangers abducting and hurting their children.

In the place where I'm from, there are no strangers. Everybody knows everybody, and kids know their molesters. My Uncle Gary liked two things: meth and little boys. My mother let him watch me almost every night. She was a dancer, gone almost all night, and didn't want to spend money on a sitter. From the age of six or seven, when he started with me, I was told to keep my mouth shut and everything would be okay.

He always started with, "Wanna have some fun?"

I left when I couldn't take any more of his fun. I left after I hit him on the head with a pan and left him lying bleeding and unconscious. I hope that I killed him. But I also hope that I will never know. The strangest thing about leaving the only world that you have ever known is the fact that you find out how your family and home life really measure up to others. I guess it was no surprise to find out that it wasn't ideal, the way that I grew up. But it made me who I am now.

I sit in alleys, on sidewalks, and in open-air restaurants. I empty half-filled coffee cups and eat the food that others had no use to finish. You sleep when you can, and you stay where they let you stay. But it is what it is, for now. Matty often tells me how he is going to do good things with his life. He always says that he will bring Jana and me along. A few months of being together and we have a bond. In the area where we stay, we're the three youngest people there. The homeless seem to age at an exponential rate.

Rick is a veteran; two tours, he always says—strangely, I don't know where he toured. All I know is when we sleep near him, he has a lot of nightmares. He's in his 30s, but he looks gaunt, ragged, and aged. He's a tall, dark-haired, angry man. But he looks fifty if he looks a day.

Matty still looks young, but the streets are taking their toll. Jana is tall, maybe 5 foot 7 or 8 inches, and she has a sort of stocky build. She has strawberry-blonde hair and the sweetest voice. I think, under other circumstances, she would have been a singer.

Some nights, I lay on the ground and think of Jana giving a concert. Maybe a medium-sized hall, three to five hundred people. A pianist plays a mix older and newer tunes, and she croons them like the records that my mom would listen to in her room when she was home. A bit of Nina Simone or Diane Krall. Her hands holding the microphone stand, and she leans back with her eyes closed and raises her voice to the heavens. As the song ends, she waves her right hand over the audience as if to say, "This is all for you."

I know that sooner or later, we'll all lose contact. It happens out here on the streets. The condition, as it is, dictates that we must find our own ways. I don't know what happens to my friends from here, but I do know that no matter where you are in this world, you are alone.

My life, whatever it may be worth, is a pile of nothing. I find no pleasure in it. I hadn't since my uncle started partying with me. I'm not sure how much of the pain I live with is my uncle's doing and how much just came naturally, but my mental state is garbage.

I don't see anything beyond being here. Living where I can, eating and drinking when I find things that I can consume. I'm at the bottom of the ladder. I look up constantly, not because I like birds or buildings. I look up because maybe there is a God.

I don't think there really is, but if there is, why can't he help me?

I cry a lot. I try to do this where no one can see or hear me. I think that Matty has heard me a few times lately; he's been a bit different torward me. Being "fatherlier," I guess. But I just keep heading down my path.

My life, for the bit that it may be worth, is a

waste. Maybe the lenses that I use to see this world are cloudy, maybe they were never my prescription, but they're what I have. If I ever leave, what would I be?

I wake and feel the morning on my face—the chill, the biting chill from a foggy morning. I walk to the waterfront and think again of leaving here and the future and it comes to me in an instant.

No. I'm never leaving. There is nothing for me out there. I have no place to call home. Going back south would be a mistake. Leaving Washington would be difficult because I have no money. So, I stay on these streets, getting old before my time. I don't do drugs; I drink liquor when I can get my hands on it. I think most teenagers are deeper into illegal activities than I am. But I bet that I have most of them beat on assaults with a deadly weapon. Not a good thing, but it's what I've got. I once heard in school that "no man is an island."

At 13, I didn't exactly understand what was being said. I took it at face value. You know, no one stands alone in this life.

As I sit on this pier and look over the water, I get it now. It's not that no one stands alone, but it's that if we stay still, if we don't swim to a safe-haven or to a shore, we'll drown in our fears, sadness, and confusion. Only islands sit out in the ocean with no fear of waves, storms, or floods; it stands forever.

I jump; no one is around to hear or see me.

No man is an island, I think as I descend into the freezing water. I never learned to swim—Maybe Alanis Morissette would add, "Jumping into the ocean with not knowing how to swim, and isn't it ironic? Don't you think?" Maybe Jana could sing it.

I don't know right now, as I look up from the

bottom of the water, if I have the energy or desire to learn how to swim. To reach for air and to any shore. Maybe I'll float to the deep end of the water. Looking up, I do realize, as everything begins to dim. I know there is no God, not for people like me. My chest hurts, and I am swallowing water. In the last moments, I find that I begin to cry. Then I laugh, no one sees tears underwater.

That Walt

The father stared blankly at the park. His children have long since grown up, and he only walks his dog here. Children and parents are still the same; children run and chase one another; they meet new friends every time they come to the park. Parents, although on their phones now, still communicate. Learn about new parents' groups in the area, clubs for their children, or maybe someone that matches their likes.

Walt's kids live in Idaho and Ohio now, far away from their parents. He and his wife had stayed in the family home in Washington. The weather was ideal for Walt's many ailments, and Nancy grew up there and still had so much family there to support them after the children moved away.

It was quaint, a small town, more of a suburb than anything else. When they moved there, everyone in the neighborhood knew one another. All the kids had grown up together. Now, as he walked home with Benny, their fifth dog in their thirty plus years together, he looked about the old neighborhood. It was all different. Sure, Walt felt safe, but most of the people he'd gotten to know over the years had sold their homes and moved to old folks' homes or those 55-plus communities.

That he and Nancy stayed was nothing short of a miracle. It was harder every day to get up the stairs to go to bed, and Benny didn't like them either. But such was life as you got older.

"Walter, is that you?" Nancy had always called him Walter, and she always asked (very loudly) if it was him.

And always the wise guy, "No, it's Benny and a burglar!"

They both laughed every time he said it, then Benny would make a run at Nancy and nuzzle her leg. It was one of the things that forty years afforded, familiarity and strong affection. Walt still walked in and gave her the usual slap on the butt and a kiss on the neck.

"Watch it, Benny, that's my girl!" This only served to slow Benny down for a minute, then he went back to harass Nancy.

"So, you two, how was the walk today?" Nancy had gone back to chopping romaine lettuce for some type of salad that she forced Walt to eat with his dinner.

"The usual, Benny's getting faster and I'm getting slower. But he's a good man for keeping me moving every day!" Walt had made his way from the treat jar to the nook table and sat down followed closely by his best bud. "Here you go, Benny! A well-deserved treat for my boy."

He was rubbing the dog's head when Nancy began to wash her hands and then she spoke a bit more softly. "Walter, the Simms' house was broken into last night."

Although Clarence and Beverly Simms had moved several years ago, they still called it the Simms' house. And hearing that there was a break-in two houses away irritated him. It was never fear when he heard these things, it was er. Why couldn't people buy their own stuff? They were weak-minded and didn't want to work. Still, he had to make conversation.

"What? The hell you say?"

"Yes, I read about it on the police blotter today." Nancy sat next to Walt, and he could tell she was afraid.

"Babe, we'll be fine. We have an alarm, security lights, and should all else fail—Benny."

They stopped and looked over at Benny as he was busying himself by chewing on his paw while lying on his back. Walt took only a moment to smile and told Nancy, "Now don't you feel safer looking at that display?"

Their laughter made Benny stop and stare at them while balancing perfectly on his back.

"Look, Nance, it's a different neighborhood. Hell, it's a completely different town now. Maybe it's time to move. Nothing is keeping us here. Your family keeps to themselves anyway. The kids are states away. We can go anywhere. What do you say?"

"But this is our home." Nancy looked sad at the thought of leaving the home where they raised their children, spent a majority of their married life, and where they had met most of their adult friends.

"I know, look, it's just a thought." Walt leaned back in his chair and gave her his best McConaughey smile. She knew that look, and it always made her smile.

"Let's wait for a while. Maybe things will change for the better."

"Sure, I don't want to leave tomorrow, it's just a thought." Walt had been mentioning this more and more.

He saw it on the walks that he and Benny took each day. Spray paint scrawled symbols everywhere, and he heard the parents at the park complain about the types of litter found in the playground areas. Between the drug paraphernalia and the liquor and beer bottles, it was not a great place. The city cleaned it daily to make it all appear like it wasn't happening, but it was there.

This morning, Walt had a couple appointments at the local VA. Benny and Nancy would have the morning to be together. As he left, he looked at the two of them and spoke to them about what they might do with their day.

"Okay, you two, no parties, no drinking, and definitely no pizza without me! I love you both." Walt blew a kiss as he walked out and headed toward his car.

At the VA, it was the usual visits. Psych appointments today—medication check-ups and therapy. It was helpful that he had stopped drinking a few years ago, and his medications were really helping him because of it. Nancy loved that the drinking, well his drunkenness, had stopped and that Benny was helping him get out more. Walt took advantage of his time in therapy these days; not just being there but being an active participant. The adage of "for it to work, you gotta do the work" had saved his life. He knew that. So, he never missed his meds and never skipped an appointment. Plus, he could talk to veterans in the canteen.

A bunch of old guys telling older stories about when they had been better than they were now. It was the most fun part of the time when he was away from home.

Between anxiety and his depression, he typically only wanted to be around Nancy, the kids, or Benny. Visiting with the guys and ladies here was a treat.

They'd been talking for about an hour when Walt said that it was time to head home. His wife and dog would be missing him. Everyone laughed at that, and he got the waves and goodbyes as he headed out.

Some of the worst moments in life get caught in your mind like a big bite of meat in your teeth. As Walt drove down the street toward their neighborhood, he saw the tagged fences and broken bottles all over the street sides. He turned into the neighborhood whistling an old Billy Joel song when the lights sent a sick wave to the pit of his stomach.

He'd called Nancy twice on the way home and she had not answered. *Please God*, he thought to himself, *let it be any other house*. But God didn't answer either. It was his home where three police cars and an ambulance were parked.

"No…no…no! What the fuck? Please, she's okay. She has to be okay," Walt said to himself as he drove up to the house.

He steeled himself for whatever was going on inside the home. Maybe she fell, maybe she cut herself cooking dinner. He had told her that the new knives were super

sharp. He parked across the street a couple houses away and stepped out of the car slowly.

"Officers, I live here. What happened?" Walt spoke calmly, but his mind and heart were going a million miles an hour.

In the distance he heard, "Let him through."

"Hello, I'm Walter Phillips. Did my wife hurt herself? I told her the new knives were too sharp." He knew police didn't respond to a cut, he knew it was far worse, what he didn't know is what exactly had happened in the house. But when they have to allow you to cross the tape, it's never a good thing. Never.

"Mr. Phillips, please sit down." The officer's name tag read Marquez.

Walt knew that nothing good ever came of "sit down."

"I'm fine standing, sir. Please just tell me what happened." Walt spoke slowly and seemed in control.

Officer Marquez took a deep breath before he spoke. "There was a break in, Mr. Phillips. It appears that your wife—"

"Where is Nancy?" He wasn't ready to hear any answer that he knew would be next, but he had to hear it now, "I need to see her right now, please."

"Mr. Phillips, your wife was killed…"

Officer Marquez continued to talk, but it was distant and muffled. Walt heard nothing clearly. The world wasn't spinning or falling away like you sometimes hear; he was in control but couldn't comprehend the words being spoken to him. It seemed like an eternity had passed when he heard the first clear words from Officer Marquez.

"Mr. Phillips, are you okay?" Marquez stopped speaking for the moment. He found a moment to let the man breathe.

"No. No, I'm not. Where is my wife? I just want to see my wife, please."

"I understand, but it would be best if you didn't see her. Not right now. Please, Mr. Phillips, she's being loaded into the ambulance now. It would be best to see her later."

"Okay, I need to go and get my dog from the back yard…" Walt was trying to hold back his tears now. At least he had Benny.

Officer Marquez's delivery of the worst news of Walt's life was not quite done. "Mr. Phillips…" It was the pause; the pause told Walt all that he needed to know. "It's just that—"

"Benny too." Walt was finally broken. The warm, uncontrollable tears flowed, and he no longer cared who saw them. It was all too much now, the world was feeling distant. His wife and dog gone; the tears, though, were of uncontrollable anger. He was quiet as the tears flowed. Expressionless, angry, and wanting revenge. No, they were tears of anger.

Marquez spoke in a sad, but controlled tone. "Mr. Phillips, your dog is also deceased. I'm really at a loss for words. We want to finish up in the kitchen and we will head out. Do you have anyone that can help you with cleaning up? We can recommend some companies if need be."

"No. I can take care of everything. I need to call our kids. We have everything taken care of. Can she go directly to Lovell's Funeral Home?"

"No, sir. There will be an autopsy first. The coroner's office will contact you, and then she can be taken to the funeral home of your choice." Officer Marquez was calm and comforting. Walt would think about it later and appreciated how well Marquez had handled the minutes after he had arrived at the house. Right now, though, he wasn't ready to give thanks and appreciation to anyone.

Walt called the boys shortly after the police and ambulance had left. It was the most painful call of his life. He was supposed to die first. Walt was the sick one, the one with all the problems. Nancy was healthy and had a long life to live. Why?

In the hours after, he was in the kitchen and had cleaned up most of the damage and blood. They never tell you what happens after the police leave a crime scene, the pain that the family members go through to clean up what the criminals did. They offer different clean-up services, but Walt needed to work through all of it. Broken glass, cabinet doors pulled off, and blood. The fucking blood was everywhere.

He cried the entire time. Walt had never been a crier, yet tonight it wouldn't stop. After finishing the cleaning, he walked to his study. He hadn't been there in a while. He had two things in there, books and booze.

The books he read on his tablet while sitting in the same room as Nancy, and the booze he had let go of for years. He sat down and stared at his impromptu bar that he had created over the years when he had been a drinker.

He sat for hours that night, staring at the liquor on the shelves. Walt just couldn't bring himself to hop off the wagon. He fell asleep in the chair wanting to hit the world.

"Dad, wake up," Dylan spoke quietly.

Walt was groggy. "Son, I… I'm sorry, I fell asleep here last night."

Dylan spoke in a condescending tone as he looked over at the liquor shelves. "Dad, did you fall asleep or pass out?"

"I understand, Dylan, but I don't drink. Not anymore."

Walt truly had put his family through the wringer with his drinking over the years. "I thought about it, but I fell asleep before I could do anything. Thank you for coming so quickly, son."

The men hugged. And Dylan began to cry into his father's shoulder. Walt, for his part, was all cried out, but he squeezed his son like he'd held him when he fell off his bike as a child. You just hold on till they let go.

Michael arrived later in the day. The three men spoke about arrangements and insurance while the spouses and grandchildren visited in the other room. When all the business of a funeral had been arranged, Walt stepped into the other room and greeted his grandchildren and daughters-in-law. The children were a bit too young to understand. The ladies were crying and spoke kindly of Nancy.

Walt thanked everyone for arriving so quickly. He was glad that he had done all the clean-up the night before. Having any one of them see what the kitchen looked like would have been devastating to them.

The coroner's office was done that afternoon, and the funeral home did a very nice job of getting things ready within a day. Nancy and Walt had been prepared for years with all of their wishes and with their plots. The only thing that they couldn't have planned for was that it would be a closed casket. It broke his heart that he couldn't remember if he told Nancy that he loved her when he walked out the last time that he had seen her alive.

It never really crosses your mind how inane a lot of your conversations are until you try to remember the last words you shared with a loved one. The most painful thing about a last conversation is trying to remember if it was something worthwhile or just wasted thoughts.

Walt hadn't remembered that animal control had arrived during the time that he had been speaking with Officer Marquez. He wasn't sure about everything that had happened, those details were yet to come.

A day or two after the funeral, the boys and their families had said goodbye. Everyone hugged, said their "I love you's" to one another. Once again, Walt was alone.

In the month that followed, Walt reached out to the police and wanted to know what had happened that day and if they had any leads. The police told him that it had been a very violent scene, and it was best that he did not know any details. Walt could not accept that and requested all the information about what had happened. He even threw in a please.

He would open the whiskey first, and after having read the report, he couldn't be sober. These animals had been so violent.

Police Report Excerpt:

"Subject, Nancy Phillips, 57-year-old female. Officers ascertain that as many as four assailants entered the home through the kitchen door. Mrs. Phillips was stabbed fifty-six times from her neck down to her legs. She was subjected to multiple blunt force

trauma to her face, back, and abdomen. She had multiple slashes
to her face, and she was almost scalped. The family dog appears to
have been subdued outside but brought inside and was hung by its
neck from a light fixture. The assailants then broke dishes,
cabinets, and windows. Footprints found are from four distinct
tennis shoes, no DNA or other evidence was located."

Twice. Walt had read the complete report twice. Looking for any hint of humanity in these men. Walt had found absolutely none. In the course of his life, he had been a good drunk but tonight wouldn't have taken much. Throughout the night, he stared at the half-filled glass, and he couldn't bring himself to do it. It would have been enough, but he had already endured every word and thought of and visualized what had happened on that night. He passed out, tired, after going over the few details of the attack listed in the police report over and over in his head.

As he lay there in a stupor of pain and anger, he recalled his dream. He was standing in the kitchen as it all happened in front of him. The knives were going in and out of Nancy as she screamed in pain and blood poured out of her. The men then held her up by her hair and slashed of most of her beautiful face and cut her forehead at the hairline and pulled it back to expose bare skull. What had actually killed her? Which wound? Which stab?

And his poor Benny, they had hit him outside, maybe with a rock. They went inside, killed the love of his life, then, when they had done that, they crafted a noose from curtains and picked his gentle giant up and tied that noose around his neck. Did they watch him struggle to breathe? Those sick fucks.

Walt woke up, groggy from his first drinks in all that sober time. He felt like he'd been run over by a giant cheese grater. Everything hurt, especially his heart. His heart and mind after a couple of weeks of feeling sorry for himself, Walt decided to call the police and find out what was happening with the search for the people that had done this to Nancy. The detective that picked up spoke calmly and authoritatively.

"Mr. Phillips, hello, thank you for calling. My name is Detective Ron Williams. I've been assigned to your wife's case. I'm working diligently to catch the people that did this, but we don't have witnesses, unfortunately your security camera doesn't save videos, and there was no DNA other than your wife's and yours found. As of right now, we are at a bit of an impasse with leads."

Walt was angry, but calm. He needed this man's help. "What does that mean, sir?"

"Mr. Phillips, your neighbors are afraid to speak. The gang violence in the area has gotten worse by the day. We could guess who it might have been, but there's no real way of making anything happen without anyone talking. We can shake some trees where our usual suspects hide, but it won't make much of a difference if no one is talking. I'm sorry, Mr. Phillips, but I don't have much to go on right now. I won't give up though; I'll contact you as soon as I have any updates. Can I help you with anything else?"

Walt knew that those words were a polite way of saying, *I need to get you off the phone, I've got cases that I can solve.* "No, thank you for taking my call, Detective."

"Okay, sir. Have a good afternoon." Walt heard a click. A moment of silence. Then a dial tone. He'd never thought that sound could make him feel so desperate. He was truly alone in this world right now and he needed to do something to save himself. In that instant, he knew what had to be done.

He stopped taking his medications that night. Walt thought that he needed to be very clear for what lie ahead over the next few weeks. He was going to find the people that took his life from him.

He would spend two weeks getting all his medicine out of his system. The PTSD medicines were to stop his nightmares and paranoia; without those, on any given day he was on edge and anxious to the point of distraction and suicidal ideations. But in his active-duty days, and now as he prepared for what he had to do, the edge would be needed as he began planning. Walt found out that rage had become his best tool; it kept him centered and beyond mere focus. He sat in the dimly lit study, staring at the liquor one last time. The liquor had never been the actual draw; it was being drunk, unaware, and uninhibited. Nancy had always taken care of him when he was drunk. She had finally talked him into letting her drive a few months after they were married. He wasn't a macho type of guy; letting his wife drive was in no way emasculating.

The next couple of weeks in addition to dropping medications, he was throwing out bottles of liquor. Each day there was a new bottle. And a step closer to getting out there to find out who had come to their home.

The nightmares of what he imagined from that afternoon were getting worse each night; the killing was becoming clearer to him. The last part was always the exposed skull and Benny hanging from the ceiling. He would wake up in tears of anger. The anger was boiling hotter each day. Walt had learned during his time in the military that a healthy bit of anger with a lot of self-control was a very dangerous combination.

Walt had never presented himself as dangerous, it was that aspect of his personality that he saved for people that needed to meet that person. In his civilian life, only two people had ever met *That Walt*. One was a man that had been yelling at not only his kid, but all of the children on the baseball field during a game when Dylan had played Little League. The other was a man that felt like being unsafe with his open carry weapon in a restaurant. The best part of the dangerous side of Walt was he was in complete control of that man. The baseball bully was sitting in lawn chair beside his minivan drinking a soda when Walt approached him. It had gone very quickly, as the man didn't appreciate being approached by anyone and tried to be tough f r o m the word go.

"What the fuck do you want? I'm trying to watch

practice." The man scowled like it was supposed to intimidate Walt.

Then, it was Walt's turn to speak. He looked around, saw no one nearby, and went into his mode. Moving deceptive quickness, he grabbed the man by his hair and spoke softly. "Keep your mouth shut." His only warning, "You were extremely rude and loud on Tuesday night at the game. I don't give a good goddamn how you talk to your son; that's your person you're fucking up. But as for my children and the children of the other parents on this team, you will never speak that way again to any one of them. Do you understand me?"

"Yes." The man was on the verge of tears from the way his hair was being pulled, and he was crushing his soda can, to keep from yelling. "Please let go."

"Are you sure you understand? I don't ever want to have this conversation again." Walt spoke calmly to the man.

"Yes. I promise, I understand."

Walt squeezed his fist full of hair for just a moment longer. He then let go and dropped a few pieces of hair onto the man's crushed soda can. He stood, smiled the type of smile the man never wanted to see again, "Clean yourself up, you have soda all over yourself."

And, just like that, he turned and slowly walked away. He had put *That Walt* away for now. The loud man never made a peep at a game again.

Walt sat in his study that now housed only books and thought of the places that he needed to try to get information. It would start with the neighbors. They knew something, those men had not been invisible. He knew that people were scared. Next, there had been no car seen in or near the neighborhood. It had been daylight, so four men walking into the neighborhood might not have been noticed.

Still, if he knew anything about Nancy, she had tried to fight. That meant the violence was ramped up to show her a lesson. That also meant that they had likely meant to rob the house, but the fight in the kitchen and Benny were more than enough to make them just destroy the kitchen and leave. Walt sat thinking, getting his plan together. No need to stall or wait any longer; he was ready to move forward.

The second visit of *That Walt* was in a local restaurant a couple of years ago. The state had become open carry. Nancy and Walt were trying a new breakfast spot. The man had a Glock hanging lazily off of the backside of his belt. The holster was not even snapped shut.

To make matters worse, the man had his back to the restaurant. Any schlub could have grabbed the weapon and made it a very bad day. Walt had a habit of eyeing dangerous things in public when he saw them. He sat facing the man's backside. Luckily, the man had gotten up to use the restroom. He was a shitkicker from some small town. A big moustache, an old trucker's hat, and jeans that would have fit him in middle school.

Walt excused himself, and when he entered the bathroom, the other Walt came out for business as he quietly locked the door. The man was loudly peeing into a urinal, one hand on the wall, the other on his hip. He never felt Walt's presence until it was a moment too late.

Walt deftly grabbed the weapon, backed away from the man to give him room to put his pecker away, spin around, and speak first.

"You're a fucking dead—"

Walt thought, *Boring.* So, he kicked the man in the stomach. The man doubled over with no air left in him. He was holding his stomach and looking toward the floor.

"Grab some air, but keep your mouth shut." Walt spoke quietly and in control. "Do you know anything about weapons safety?"

There was a moment of silence as the stunned man stared, "Oh, you can answer that one."

"Yes. Why else would I have it, asshole?" The man was still a tough guy.

"Asshole?" Walt pulled back the slide on the 9-milimeter and checked that he had a round in the chamber. "I wouldn't call the man with your weapon in his hands, round chambered, and full knowledge of how to use it an asshole. Ok, you had a 9-millimeter Glock pistol hanging off your belt like you were in the

Old West, you jackass. Do you realize how dangerous that is to everyone around you?"

"Look for yourself, I had the safety on."

"Okay, stupid, how exactly would you have stopped anyone from grabbing the weapon and running? You had your back to the restaurant with your weapon holster not snapped shut, loaded— Loaded?! You know, I walked back here to either shoot you with your own gun or speak with you about weapon safety. So, how do you want this conversation to end?"

"I'll be more careful, sir." Walt thought it was funny that people call you sir when they think you want to kill them.

"I know you will. You won't forget the day you almost died, now, will you?"

"No, sir."

Walt popped out the clip and removed the

chambered round. He then took the pistol apart and spoke slowly and very controlled, "I'll hang onto this clip and these dangerous bullets. You won't need them. And don't get your friends hurt." A very well-placed pause followed. "Put your empty weapon back together and put it into your locked holster, maybe toward the front of your belt where you have eyes and control of it. Got it?"

The man merely shook his head and didn't look up again. Walt, for his part, walked to the sink, slipped the clip into his right front pocket, and then washed his hands. He dried up and unlocked the door. He sat down, smiled at his wife, and picked up the coffee that she had ordered for him.

The man came out a bit quieter, and his weapon was not on his backside. Walt was able to finish his breakfast, and as he and Nancy left, he dropped the clip into a trashcan.

That was it, the only two times Walt had brought out his dark side. He knew he was going to have to find him again, and he hoped very soon. But it would take some work.

During Walt's time in the Army, his job allowed him to stay stateside for most of his active-duty time. He'd only been to Korea for one year. Otherwise, he had told Nancy he was a mechanic. What Walt actually did included monitoring phone conversations, conducting interrogations, and a few other things that no one but the interviewee and him would ever know. There are things that hide in plain view of the world that people never know about or choose not to notice. The whispers of their methods had always been there, but no proof. Amongst his unit, the motto was, "Guilt found by any means."

So, when asked about his service, it was stateside, Korea, and some travel. And to Nancy's recollection, Walt was the cleanest mechanic she'd ever seen. He came home clean every day; all the wives would say that about the husbands in that unit. But living a life like that also led him to want to forget many of the things that he'd done. The thing for Walt was that he was an intimidator.

That Walt scared men and women alike, the guilty had no gender in his eyes.

That Walt found guilt by any means, every single time. And when others needed a confession or a heavy hand, they called Walt. No one knew that Captain Phillips called himself *That Walt* on those occasions, but they knew something about him was extremely scary in those rooms.

Had he killed anyone? Yes. But those weren't people to him. They were traitors and victims of their own crimes, but they were not people.

It was a part of his job. The killing, the lies to

Nancy and the boys, and the lying to himself. After Dylan was born, Walt spent some time home to regroup and recharge. It was his next mission that made him decide to walk away from the unit and the military.

They were sent to Georgia in the late summer; they were greeted by the post commander's liaison and the unbearable humidity and heat.

The initial briefing was about an hour with the post commander and his staff; nothing was to leave this room. They had names and units in hand; the military police along with the mechanics would all move at the same time. It was all scheduled for fifteen hundred hours (3 p.m.). The lower-level soldiers would be arrested by the local military police; the leaders of the group would be taken into custody by the mechanics. All cellphones would be confiscated before any calls of warnings could be made.

There was an extremist group that had started

up amongst several soldiers, with talk of eliminating soldiers of different colors and races. There were eyes on it, but at the time it was considered to be contained. When the mechanics arrived, there were about thirty soldiers amongst six units in separate battalions that had become involved.

Squashing this now was top priority. Walt, the senior man on the ground, was tasked with interrogating the leaders. The first two soldiers were not forthcoming at first, then *That Walt* decided to finish the interview.

Within an hour, Walt knew everything that they knew. They volunteered information that neither the mechanics nor any other part of the military had yet known—Even Walt thought it had been a very effective interrogation. That's why he got the big bucks, his leadership would say later. The thing about having volunteered all that information: they couldn't very well go back out to the general public. So, they were "reassigned" to another unit. That was mechanic speak for "not to be seen again" by anyone. There were promises for them and their families of relocation and protection.

Their cover? They were sent on a mission to begin the ruse. But all it was for them was a short walk down a dark hallway, a free bullet to the back of the skull, and permanent deletion by the mechanics. It was explained that the mission, after being discovered by some of their former friends had been compromised and before they were able to leave post. It was with sincere apologies and regrets to the families for the government's failure in being able to protect them.

As for benefits, the initial reason no benefits would be payable to any of their family was the trouble that they had incurred before being sent away. Again, apologies were offered and the doors were closed behind them. The mechanics, if nothing, were very thorough; all the moves were thought of before feet were on ground. No excuses or mistakes were accepted by Walt's unit.

The people not in the military that had been implicated would be contacted by federal authorities that had no affiliation with the military. But before Walt could leave, he had been given the name of a big fish that needed to be interviewed about the group. The name dropped by both detainees was Major Annette Davidson. Davidson had been in the Army for fifteen years and had been successful at every level. Many awards and commendations to her name; she had been the executive officer here for just over one year. But how long had she been doing what the men had accused her of doing?

On the way to the office, his men joked that he

would be getting the first "Twofer" of the quarter. The woman was not expecting the visit from Walt, and that was to his advantage. He walked in, quietly locking the door; her work phone had been shut off just before he walked in, and her cellphone lost signal as he locked the door. Her commander had been briefed with only the information that he needed. There was nothing that would happen outside of her office, and it would all be taken care of discreetly.

"Don't speak, Mrs. Davidson. I'm here to speak with you about allegations made by soldiers that you are part of an extremist group here on this post. Now, what is your involvement?"

Walt was met with silence; then she attempted to use her cellphone and then picked up her work phone. He took those moments to sit in a chair across from her. Realizing that neither was working, she sank into her work chair and started trying to think of a lie.

"Speak now." Walt was almost there, but he was holding back, hoping that she would be reasonable.

"I have no—" She started off with a negative, meaning that she was about to lie.

"I'll stop you there. By using the word 'no,' I'm led to believe that you are about to throw 'idea' plus some other BS behind the word 'no'. Which is a lie. I don't like to be lied to. I'm not a person that you want to lie to under any circumstance. Please, believe that." Walt was now the only calm one in the room.

Her lip had started to sweat, her eyes were becoming dilated as she was beginning to panic, and she had pursed her hands together squeezing the handles like a stress ball. All signs that she was becoming very stressed.

"I think I might need—" she started to speak,

but he knew what she wanted.

"Stop." Walt spoke in a disconcertingly calm tone, "You will not get help from anyone outside of this room--until you answer my questions. Not a doctor, an attorney, your priest. No one is coming into or out of this room until we finish talking."

"I know my rights, Captain!" she said indignantly.

"You have no rights, Mrs. Davidson." He said with a half-smile and matter of fact; then he shifted in the chair and crossed his right leg over his left—this was simply another move to make him look too calm. Then, the smile faded. And he began with what he needed to say, pausing for a brief moment then beginning to speak. "You gave up your rights and military career when you helped recruit soldiers for a Nazi group based out of Ohio." Another pause because she needed to be aware of what he knew. "Now, what you will tell me, and in short order, is when this started, who are your contacts, and where we will find them."

Davidson wanted to stall; maybe Captain Phillips didn't know, for sure, as much as he led on. How much could she bank on him really knowing?

So, she bluffed. "This is illegal. Locking me in a room alone, no female officer to monitor my safety. And then, you try to intimidate me with a bunch of made-up allegations. I won't stand for this. I will sue the Army and you, specifically, over this. My attorney is going to have a field day with you."

"Are you done, Ms. Davidson?"

No answer. The color was draining from her face, no one was coming to save her, it was his demeanor that made her feel, almost, queasy—he was too damn calm.

Walt stood, his mind was on the very edge of stepping off of the bridge. It didn't take much when he was ready to get down to real work. This individual had used the military to recruit white soldiers in various corners of the world to join a group that she was elbows deep into. It was amazing how much intel people gave you when their lives were on the line. The only thing that he liked about this game was wondering exactly how long it would take to make her break. Speaking with his buddies prior to heading into the office, he guessed once he got to business it would be seven minutes. So, he raised his wrist and looked at his watch. Seven minutes and counting. Time to go to work.

"I let you finish that line of bullshit since you were just trying to gauge what I know. I'll end the game there because I'm not in the mood. You've assisted in bringing at least forty individuals into that organization. It began when you were stationed at Fort Sam Houston about ten years ago. One of your former commanders talked you into it."

Walt didn't use notes or paper; he wanted the detainee to believe that he was very well versed in the case. He was knowledgeable and confident in what he knew about the individual in front of him.

"A hint for you, Mrs. Davidson, they choose the weak-minded people, as they are the easiest to control. We both know that don't we? So, Lt. Col. Roderick Michaels brought you into the organization."

He saw her wince when she heard the name. It might not go for the full seven minutes. Only five and a half minutes to go.

"You were his girlfriend, and he used you to recruit younger soldiers. After you moved from there, it appears that you stayed in contact, and you continued the work all over our country." Walt would then pause and strategically scratch his forehead, like he was thinking. It was a diversion tactic really. "Mr. Michaels was picked up earlier today from his home in Wisconsin. In front of his wife and children."

It was little facts along the way, like where Michaels was now living, that made Walt that much more effective. Four minutes left on the clock.

"Now, you betrayed your country, your commission as an officer, and your oath as a soldier. There is no path back for you. So, it's your turn to talk?"

She took a long breath. "I need some protection if I'm going to speak about anyone."

And there it was. He glanced at his watch; it took three minutes and forty-five seconds to break her. It was now time to cuff her and take her down that same dark hallway so many had walked beforehand. As she stood up to be handcuffed, he saw her pregnant belly for the first time. He knew that he would have to see it, but with Nancy at home with Michael in her belly, this one would prove difficult. But it was his job, right?

She was ushered out of the building into a tiny government van with no windows. This would be as close as she would ever get to the hallway. She was placed in the second seat back and cuffed to it. Walt, for his part, sat directly behind her.

"Look, I need to call my boyfriend. He'll be worried about me and I'm due in just a couple of weeks." Davidson knew she was in trouble but was trying to get things arranged before the shit hit the fan over the next few days.

She sat, thinking to herself, how embarrassed her family would be. Imagining her daughter being born while she was locked away awaiting a trial. She wondered out loud, trying to get a sense of her level of trouble, maybe if she plead guilty and tried to cut a deal she would be out really soon.

As she was making plans in her mind, the man directly behind her had left and *That Walt* had arrived as only he could do the job that was necessary. She was not paying attention as he unholstered his weapon and added a silencer to it. He screwed it onto the barrel slowly as he listened to her babble. He saw her take a breath to speak, and he didn't want to hear another word about her child, trial, etc.

Walt would have heard the question, "Where are we going?" Instead, she died on inhale as she prepared to speak. It was Walt's last kill while in the military. Something about knowing that the child in her stomach was viable and could be saved with medical attention bothered him. It shut him down. For the first time in his career, *That Walt* was gone almost immediately. He could smell gunpowder and blood as he slowly removed the silencer. The world was quiet. A quiet only regretful souls can hear. Walt had never heard this quiet. Over and over, he had done this many times before, but knowing his wife sat at home with child only a few weeks from arriving made it all too real. The quiet ebbed around him for what seemed like an eternity.

He put his weapon away in its holster and locked it. Then he leaned over the seat, resting his elbows along the top. He stared at her lifeless body for a moment; he blinked hard as, for a brief moment, he thought that he saw her belly move. The thought that he couldn't stop at that moment was simple, was he watching her child die? Was that even possible?

As he continued to stare at the woman's lifeless stomach, the van lurched to a stop. He had arrived at the temporary area of operations. He had a moment. He took a flask out (later he would think that it was that exact moment that started his alcoholism), hammered down two large swallows and quickly packed it away. The van's sliding door flew open.

"Mr. Twofer!" He was greeted by his cohorts with the name—strangely, he had made that name up when it first happened; that is taking out a pregnant detainee. The mechanics were all too happy to see him having wound up this trip on a high note.

They had extinguished the entire group from this post. Every takedown had gone as planned; no one got a call off to warn anyone else. They had gotten enough intel to track down former military and current soldiers that were involved in this disturbing new trend. No news of any of the detainees had left post. Similar takedowns at posts all over the Country were coming up in the next day; the hammer would fall swiftly and with force. Overall, it had been an extremely successful week.

Walt thought about the journey's end; taking out

Davidson and her unborn child had been the icing on the cake as far as everyone else was concerned. Over and over, he heard that no one else would have done it, no one else could have done it.

But that was it for Walt. After he arrived home, he was plagued with nightmares about Nancy being shot and Michael struggling for life inside her. It started the same way each time; a mysterious figure would pull a trigger; Nancy hits the ground and Walt runs to her. He turns her over only to see the exit wound going through her face. He looks down and sees tiny hands pushing, scratching the inside of his mother's stomach. The child, begging for air, but Walt is unable to get the baby out. The scratching and pushing grow to a feverish pace; then moments later it simply stops. That was the worst feeling, Walt woke up feeling useless and nauseous. He never cared or dreamt about the people that he'd ended—never. But when it started causing dreams of his own wife and unborn child; it was something that he couldn't turn off. Walt knew in his heart that his career was over.

Soon after, he would resign his commission. He would walk away, healthy and happy to do so. His only problem was that the alcohol had gotten control of him. Sure, he would typically wait until the boys and Nancy went to bed to get really hammered, unless he was at a party. So, it was not seen by too many people as a big problem. It mainly occurred in the dead of night. He still functioned all right during the day.

He did a few different things over the years, just to get out of the house. His pension and disability took care of everything. After the boys had left, he decided to stay home. Leaving the house every day had become quite difficult. He couldn't see himself doing anything for any extended period of time.

Plans, events, or appointments all bothered him in ways that he had never imagined. The regimented life of a soldier and what his missions were, had pushed him to stay dangerously focused. He left it at work when he was still a soldier, but now the missions were over. Walt felt useless and that struck him in the form of anxiety.

Much of life, outside of spending time with Nancy and calling the boys seemed far too difficult. He started going to therapy at the VA; for the first time in his life, he'd admitted that he needed help. It wasn't dreams or memories that drove him there; the driving force was the fact that he was drowning himself in alcohol. Sure, if he was on the stand testifying, he would have to say that he remembered every kill, every second of every moment spent interrogating detainees—he was too much of a chickenshit to call them people or soldiers. All of those moments were stacked up in his consciousness, and they ate him up when he was sober.

That is what he finally learned in therapy. Not the hippie stuff people talk about, but real healing. Real expression and healing. No details in group, but a lot of heavy thinking and sharing. His therapist, Dr. William Bradley (Billy as Walt would later begin calling him) had saved Walt from himself and also Walt's relationship with his family. The most important part of therapy is the work the patient is willing to do, the choices made on a daily basis. One day, one step at a time…

Nancy never had the opportunity to tell him how proud she was that he got help with his mental health, or that he stopped drinking. Those were two things that Walt never knew.

He'd turned the chair in the study toward the window. He'd been here for a while. Going through his life. Finding out if he still had *That Walt* somewhere in him for one more ride. Even if he could find him, he was much older. Would he be as quick as he needed to be? Could he be as mean and angry with the same control?

He found that the neighbors did know a lot more than they wanted to share with the police. Apparently, they were afraid of the gangs that came in from the city. It had become a pastime of theirs, it seemed. Getting the information was all about playing good cop, interrogate to learn was a trick he had learned as a mechanic. He would assure the neighbors that he would only use any information he gathered to give to his detective and no other names would be provided to the police or anyone else.

Cops were slower to respond in the small towns, fewer security systems, and once you found a good area, you could work it for a while. Walt found out that a Latin gang known as the Eastside Emperors had chosen his neighborhood as their personal turf. They didn't have any names or descriptions; they had heard this from a friend of a friend whose husband was a cop.

Walt knew speaking to him was difficult and he thanked them. It was time to do some homework of his own. But he would need better internet access than the normal person. He had kept up with some of his co-workers over the years, more to heal himself than anything else. But he knew that plenty of them had gone into private international security, and they would have the type of access that he needed for what would happen next.

He reached out to Murray, a stand-up guy; they were in the same unit for a few years. Murray answered on the first ring.

"Cap! How ya' been?" Murray sounded as young

as ever.

"Good, Murray. And you? How is your family?" Walt wasn't typically much for conversations, but right now he needed a friend's ear as well as information.

"All grown up, Walt. The kids are moved away. Bernice is tired of me working. I'll probably end it soon enough. How are Nancy and the boys?"

"The boys are doing well." There was a pause, a dent in the armor that Murray had never heard before.

"Walt," full of concern for his old friend, "what's going on?"

"Nancy's gone. She was taken out in a home invasion a couple months ago," Walt spoke slowly and in control.

"Aww, Christ, Walt. I'm so sorry. Are you okay?"

"It happened during the day. I wasn't home, and

no, I'm not fucking okay."

"What do you need from me, Cap?" Murray's voice slipped back into that of a soldier, at the ready to do what needed to be done.

"I need any intel that you can get me on a gang named the Eastside Emperors out of Tacoma. Names, addresses, known hangouts, everything, the gamut."

"You got it." Murray spoke with no hesitation as he scribbled some notes. "I'll forward a secure file within the hour. Do you need any weapons? I have guys in your area."

Walt thought for a brief moment. "Thank you, I'll look for the file. And no, I won't need any weapons. Phil, thank you, my friend."

It was Murray's turn to pause. Walt had only ever   called him by his last name. "You're welcome, Walt, and God speed."

Within an hour, a large secure file arrived in an old email server that Walt knew he could trust. He read on into the night, cataloging names, addresses, distinguishing marks and tattoos, and a hierarchy of their chain of command. By morning, he had everything that he needed to begin his search for the men that had entered his home.

Having been in the military, he knew that the strongest parts of a rotting tree were the roots. They held all the nastiness above them up from falling down. So, chop at the roots to get all that rotten tree to fall.

Now the footwork. He didn't want to make any of this last any longer than necessary. Not too much into his research he found a name that showed promise. It was a young man named Cesar Gomez, eighteen years old, and he didn't know his ass from a hole in the ground. He joined the Emperors only a couple of months ago; he was still healing from being jumped into the gang. The Emperors' color of choice was brown. They said it was for Brown Pride, an idea that brought in the members. Sadly, they really only cared about green money. But Cesar was bringing in more money than he'd ever seen; he told his parents he'd found friends at his new job, and things were getting better. He was in hopes of seeing his family very soon. So, it didn't bother him at all to do some of the things that he was doing; the money would at least make him look like he was doing well for himself.

Cesar lived with a couple buddies in a small apartment. The building looked like a wreck, but they had internet, a gaming system, and weed. Walt sat for a few minutes and watched the apartment.

He was done watching, only two men were home and one of them was Cesar. Walt took a deep breath, glanced in the rearview mirror. He couldn't see him, he'd never had to think to bring *That Walt* out for business. He got out of the car, looked around carefully. And like a suit that always fits just right; he was in *that* mode when he knocked on the door.

"Go away! We already donated…" He heard laughs.

He knocked again, and this time he heard someone get up. The door opened about two inches before the man opening it got a mouthful of door. He landed covering his face and whimpering in pain. Walt stomped on his face; it wasn't Cesar, so this guy could go to sleep. He heard someone speak from another room.

"Who was it? Wrong number?" The man was obviously high. Walt peered into the room and saw his mark. The best thing about this moment was that

Cesar thought he was waiting for a friend to come back into the room. The element of surprise is your best friend on this type of mission.

Walt kicked the door open and swiftly put a boot on Cesar's face. He would go secure Cesar's roommate and then prepare for Cesar to wake up. It was only five minutes, but he needed Cesar to be aware of what was happening.

The younger man began to stir. "Wake up, Cesar. I need to speak with you."

"I know my rights, man. You can't come into my house like that! That's why I hate fucking cops!" Cesar spoke like the tough guy that he was not. In Walt's mind, it was time to go to work.

"Lucky for me, I'm not a cop. I'm a guy that does what a cop can't do. I'm the guy that comes when the law can't get around the rules. When witnesses know what is happening, they don't talk to cops. But they will talk to me. And people have been talking."

Cesar looked at the old man for a moment; the calmness of his voice was creepy. It was like something from a horror movie.

"What are you talking about, man? I don't know nothing about nothing. I'm new…" Cesar wasn't sounding as tough. Business was picking up and he had the right one.

"Oh, I think you will know enough. For me, that is. There was a murder, a woman and a do—" There it was. Walt felt it immediately. Cesar knew. The sudden, almost imperceptible tightening of the chest. He knew the scumbags that did this. They had bragged to the others about what they had done. It was time to ramp it up just a bit more.

Walt wasn't sure if he could physically do what he wanted, but he lifted the boy from the ground and threw him against a wall, caught him on a bounce and threw him onto his makeshift TV stand and through the TV.

"Cesar, you should never play poker, you don't have the demeanor for it. Now, I'll give you one chance tell me what you know about who it was that did this and where I can find them. If you choose not to cooperate, it will be a very, very long day and it will only end when I let it end. And it doesn't matter to me if you are screaming the information that I want or we are speaking like I am right now. Your move."

Cesar was a bruised teenager that had been kicked out of his parents' home for smoking weed when he was 16. A guy that had no hope for a future until he met with and joined the Emperors. He thought that he had found family. That is, until they beat him just over one month ago to make him a brother. And right now, he was just a gopher, at the bottom of the totem pole. He had no reason to protect any of them. But what if it was a test?

Cesar knew to never trust anyone but his boys. And his boys might be testing him. Then he thought of a quick lie.

"No, man. They don't tell me nothin'. I'm just a guy that sells some weed."

"All right, Cesar. I'm going to tell you something so that you understand me." The voice was like ice and pierced Cesar's thoughts, "In battle, there are those on the frontline, then there are those that back them up, and those that hang back and hope to stay safe. Now, those on the frontline, they aren't always the best—it's their job to be there. The ones hanging back, they aren't always the weakest, because if everyone gets taken, they will stay there and hold down the fort when no one else is there to take charge. Then there are the guys out there in the middle. And they have very difficult tasks. They can retreat or they can push forward. Now, here is the moral of the story. If you walk to the front line and then you see someone running toward you, toward the danger, you should be very afraid of that person. Because they are not crazy or scared of what is ahead; they intend to inflict as much damage on you, and your little friends, as possible. And they will stop at nothing to accomplish that final task."

Cesar was confused and scared. "What do you mean?"

That Walt spoke slowly.

"I ran toward you, I found you, and unless I get my answers in the next few moments, I will inflict pain upon you as you can survive. And then, I will continue until I'm tired and then I can find someone else that will talk to me."

So, Cesar spoke quickly; he knew right away that

this was no test. "It was four of the headhunters. They live on McKinley near a school. It's Eduardo, Edgar, Javier, and Felipe. There are at least ten guys that live there, but those four are the ones that did that job."

"Wow, Cesar, you did do a good job," Walt spoke soothingly, he did not want to seem as intimidating for a moment. He wanted Cesar at ease for the next few moments, and he wanted to finish up there quickly. Cesar gave him the address of the house where he would find the men. He explained that t h e y were called headhunters because they looked for new areas to rob and would work them until they had gotten what they could. They were vicious, and that's why no one told on them. Walt scooted close to Cesar and thanked him for his help. The last thing Cesar would do, in his sad life, was smile.

Walt was sad for just a moment, as he saw the young man lying still. Sadly, having believed that if you did what an authority figure told you to do, you wouldn't get punished for it. What he was, sadly, was disillusioned with life and misguided. It only took a moment to stab him and cleanly cut jugular vein with a small twist of the wrist. The boy couldn't do anything; he just smiled and went to sleep. Walt stared at the boy for just a moment, no tough guy, Eastside Emperor, or any other thing. It was a little boy that had trusted Walt. It was just Walt for the moment, just Walt. He hadn't felt this since Davidson. But he had gotten the information needed; he stood then wiped his blade on the young man's shirt and got back on task.

Before he left, he took care of the roommate, then piled the men together in their bathtub and set them ablaze. It was common practice to get rid of some of the finer evidence. After burning, he put out the flames and poured bleach over them. It would kill the smell for much longer than really needed, but this is what Walt did to even further muddy the trail of evidence. Because the apartment was in a seedy location no one would have seen anything, but the third roommate would arrive sooner than later. He quickly locked the bathroom door and left.

The third roommate's eventual arrival back home meant everything would have to happen today. Walt needed to slip back into his mode, he wasn't too sure that he could do this again. The pile of memories from his past—and now the present—were stacking up higher than he would like. Could he still continue down the rabbit hole? The real question though was even clearer.

How long can you really go on killing, Walt? He had asked himself that question dozens of times while in the Army. Earlier in life, though, he didn't care to answer it. It was rhetorical. He may as well have been shooing a fly from his watermelon on a hot summer's day; they just come right back to it, the same as Walt was to killing.

Walt walked out of the apartment and just strolled to his vehicle. The best way to not draw attention to yourself is to just walk. You don't look around darting your head and eyes or bury your hands deep into your pockets. The biggest failure in looking casual is trying to look casual.

After arriving at his target, he sat in his car, waiting for all ten men to arrive. He found it again, back in his mode by thinking and planning. Thinking of how each man's life would be ended. By the time all of them arrived, they had died in Walt's head at least ten times each. Of course, things never go the way you plan. And he honestly didn't mind that; the unexpected makes you feel that much more alive; thinking on the fly puts him on the edge that he needed. Walt would walk in with nothing more than a few knives. He couldn't have a bullet come back to any weapon that he owned. Besides, these fools would likely have plenty of guns for him to choose from when things got going in the house.

As he prepared to leave his car, he took a moment to look into the rearview mirror. He'd never done that in preparation for a mission; it took him a moment, but he saw him. *That Walt* was staring back at him. He had never liked that man; how he thought and acted, but their combined power was very dangerous. *That Walt* did things Walt would never do. He had discovered that side of him long before the military.

As a sophomore in high school, he had been bullied by some kid. One afternoon, as Walt sat in his backyard, that jackass had jumped the fence and gotten in Walt's space. It started calmly but went bad very quickly. He said something to the effect of Walt liking to suck cock; followed up with Walt being pushed to the ground. The guy then pulled his dick out, waving it in Walt's face. That was the first time *That Walt* had shown up.

Walt scooted back, then sent a foot into the boy's chest. The boy hit the ground, Walt hopped up and attacked. Sure, didn't have the tools that the Army would give him, but the rage was there, and he used it. He put his heel onto the boy's exposed dick. As he was about to scream, Walt dropped his shoe on the boy's chest, driving all the wind from his body. Walt stood back and looked about his yard; he found an old board and picked it up. It was rotten, but it did the job. The boy lay there with two of his ribs broken.

"Fuck!" Walt was a million neurons of hate and he wanted to look for something else. Then he heard the boy speak.

"Please, I'll never bother you again," he wept weakly. "Please, Walter. Please."

Walt, for his part, looked down and saw that the boy couldn't and wouldn't fight back. But he gave him a warning. "If you ever look at me or talk to me again, I'll feed you your dick. Do you understand?"

End of bullying.

Now, he was stepping from a vehicle, ready to feed each man inside that building their own dicks. *That Walt* loved to have those thoughts. He laughed quietly. It would have disturbed him on any other occasion, but not tonight.

The thing about entering a home and surprising people is that you have to come from an angle they aren't expecting you to come from. He'd studied the house for a few hours, and these men were so convinced that they were untouchable, Walt might have been able to walk in the front door. Still, there was a window on the west side of the house with no screen and they kept it open. And no one had gone into that room for at least an hour and a half. That was his way into the party.

He walked slowly across the street; he was definitely not as fast, and his bones creaked a lot. The only things that might give him any advantage were his fighting skills and the moments of surprise if he could get in that window quietly.

His memories were often difficult. He'd been a shit father. Drinking every night to escape bad memories, staying drunk throughout each weekend. Sure, he was there, but you're never really present when your mind isn't there. And that had been one of his biggest regrets. Wasting over twenty years of marriage and the youth of his children by being wasted most of the time.

The last five years had been the best of their marriage. He'd gotten to know the boys that much better, and he felt healthier than ever. Of all the dogs they ever had, Benny got the best from him—walks, attention, playtime.

Dumping the booze had been really smart. He'd never have started his path to this house had he drowned his sorrows in gin. He didn't mind guns, not since becoming very familiar with safety and handling of all types while in the Army. He might've even eaten a bullet if he'd stayed drunk. They call liquor a depressant, but until you've lost everything that matters to you and you're full of booze, you don't understand the depths that the mind can reach.

His lowest lows had come while drunk. Nancy always attempted to keep him going; she'd always been stronger than him. It hurt her deeply (and he knew it) that he kept returning to the drink. When he had finally stopped, he didn't make a fuss the night he had his last drink. The truth was, he didn't know it was his last drink until the next evening when he entered his study to grab his usual. He poured and stared. He sat down and stared at the bourbon at the bottom of his glass.

Interestingly, he just couldn't drink it. Nothing appealed to him about what was in his hand. No, it was not a conscious decision at all. It just finally clicked to him that you cannot run away from yourself. No matter how fast you run, how deep you sink into a bottle or sit brooding, you can never escape the past.

Those were the moments of your life, the totality of your experiences. And you live and die with those. Active alcoholics and drug addicts can't understand that aspect of continuing addiction. True, once you're an addict of any kind, you are always an addict.

The differences come in finding some way to control your demons.

He was feet from starting what he felt would certainly be his final mission. He'd use their guns if that time came. Depending on the room he entered, he'd have pots and pans or a toilet lid to help him on his way. Oh, the fun of entering a building with no idea where you were landing.

As luck would have it, he was in the kitchen; pots, pans, and knives—oh my.

He grabbed a few steak knives, a couple cast-iron pans, and, as an afterthought, some butter knives. Now, when you are entering an unknown terrain, there are a few things to remember:

1. The enemy is at a tactical advantage at all times.

2. Stealth is your only friend.

3. You kill at every opportunity; no one is special or saved for last—the real world doesn't have a final boss. Everyone dies when they meet him.

The men downstairs were having a heated debate about who was the best fighter in the house, how many of them had been with a girl named Rita, and why West Coast weed was the best. Walt couldn't look into the room, but it sounded like at least five distinct voices. That meant that at least half of the men would be upstairs. The television volume was going to offer a bit of help for the start.

He had been in his mode for a bit, but he would spend an extra moment preparing his mind. If this were his final go with *That Walt* then he was leaving everything there. After tonight, they would never be together again. He couldn't be there again. It hurt, these days, to be him. It was actually how Walt had come to think of *That Walt*; he was a separate entity. He was there to finish the work when Walt couldn't.

In his mind's eye, he saw Nancy. *One last time, old boy, into the breech,* he thought. And there he was. *That Walt* licked his lips and smiled his half smile. It was frightening at first, it hadn't felt this strong since he had started with his unit. It had been their second or third mission together. One of his friends was killed while trying to get intel. Walt was onsite and saw it happen. He then took it upon himself to exact revenge for what had happened.

Walt thought it was all over for him for what he did. Instead, the company CO called an informal officers' meeting. He had said that it was about time someone grew a pair and took the initiative to do what needed to be done to get things right. After that night, the unit's mission and their motto changed. They would no longer have trouble getting confessions and making them stick.

Back in the kitchen, it was time to move. He would only be able to surprise this crew once. *That Walt* flew in with his elbows bent and held tight to his body. He had hit the first man squarely in the temple, knocking him out, before any of the others even moved. His grace surprised him. Man two and three got the tops of their heads cracked open before they stood all the way up.

The final two men did stand up and were reaching for guns. The shorter man wearing pressed khaki shorts and an oversized t-shirt was farther away. As Walt ran toward them, he caught the taller man with the pan that was in his right hand while using everything he had to get his left leg up high enough to kick the shorter man in the chest. Four down. This one would take a moment; he didn't want to use a pan. He placed the pans on the couch, pulled out a steak knife, and sliced the man's throat from ear to ear. He kneeled over him for a brief moment, then shoved the steak knife through the roof of his mouth and into brain. *Lights out, motherfucker.*

Since he wasn't sure who was who and didn't really have time to find out, he looked around and found a couple of long extension cords. Two extension cords, each cut in half—in simple math, four men and four ways to choke them before they ever woke up.

In making sure that the men never woke up, he had to be sure that the plug-in part of the garrotes that he was making covered the windpipe. Just using the cord alone wouldn't crush the airway like he wanted. The extra part of the cords would secure their arms behind their backs. With a lack of air, the body would try to wake up and untie the garrote. The only way he could be sure they didn't do that was securing their hands. Was it cruel or overkill? Not to *That Walt,* not for his final mission.

That Walt would make his way up the stairs—five down, five to go. He smiled at the thought. But there were problems with going upstairs; again, where would they be? He had a steak knife in each hand. It was time to end the night.

Sometimes, he thought, *"You get lucky."* This was his night: at the end of the hall, he heard a gathering of men. Five distinct voices, just what he needed. He steeled himself for the last lunge. A couple of deep breaths—not just a breath you take to relax; no, these were jumping into the deep end of the pool and trying to swim all the way across under the water breaths.

One breath out, second breath out... It was the second bedroom on the right, and the door was already open just a bit. With lungs full of air, an empty brain, and a body skilled enough to destroy any gathering of five men, he kicked the door open and quickly scanned the layout while continuing to move forward.

The thing that many don't realize about using knives is that angles are your best friend. God made the body's most precious parts, or what Walt often referred to as "instant disablers," to be hidden behind protectors. The key to his skills with knives was knowing the proper angle to stab or cut at.

If you went at someone's heart, it was covered by a hard sternum, and you must come at them to do two things. First, you have to miss the sternum, and second, you have to pierce an artery. The lower artery carries oxygen-rich blood to the lower extremities, and the upper coronary artery takes blood upstairs. Stabbing there and twisting will easily disable someone and kill them really quickly with no medical attention. Stab and twist in the kidneys; again, it'll be lots of bleeding and quite disabling.

But *That Walt* wasn't quite that dramatic. There were other cuts that caused much more bleeding, and fast. Many people didn't understand that the carotid, brachial, and femoral arteries could make a person bleed out very quickly. So, he had to move as quickly as he could.

The best way to make everything go smoothly was to simply sever a part of the cervical spine (the back of the neck; again, with his skills, he knew exactly where) and hit one of those arteries. The carotid was best since he already had a knife by the neck.

He burst into the room. The men were congregated in the center. He didn't even see the first man's face; he severed the cervical spine and quickly severed the carotid. There was only one gun, that he could see, in the room it was placed on a TV tray in the middle of their circle. They had been playing cards and smoking weed when Walt had entered.

Their friend lay on the floor, unable to move and quickly bleeding out. There was a dirty carpet that covered the floor; otherwise, Walt may have slipped when moving forward. Having to move quickly and improvise, he kicked the TV tray with the gun as hard as he could into the face of the unlucky man farthest from him. That man had drawn the short straw for being dealt with last.

Man number two caught a blade to his neck and began to shoot out blood. Walt turned to the next closest to him and stabbed at an angle at the left side of the sternum, first piercing the lower, then up through the upper arteries. He twisted for more effect.

All the men had closely shorn hair, so Walt couldn't grab hair, but the next best thing was loose clothing. The fourth man up was grabbed by the collar of his oversized t-shirt. Walt yanked him back and dumped him on his ass. The young man, probably all of twenty, was crying. What he didn't know was that the machine above him didn't care about his tears.

That Walt used one knife to cut the carotid on the left side of his neck, and with his left hand he came down with all his force and pinned the man's head to the floor. He stood and breathed for a moment, then took a quick count. Yes, one to go. Number five had caught the TV tray to the face and was lying there still stunned and clutching his bloody nose. He was just becoming aware of what had just happened to his buddies.

It was in that moment that a laugh came from the older man walking up to the final gang member who was on his ass crying on the floor. What the gang member thought was another couple of knives that the man was pulling out of his back pocket was almost right. before he could even move, the killer was upon him with deceptive speed, punching him as hard as he could.

That Walt pulled out the butter knives and took his time. Walt had once heard of the death of a thousand cuts. He'd never tried it, he was always in a hurry, but as he stared about room, he saw that the others had bled out nicely and he time to focus on the tenth man. Walt had been a student of anatomy. He'd always wanted to try this but had never taken the time.

With just the right a n g le, he severed the larynx and destroyed the vocal cords, carefully missing the carotid artery. The young man woke up tried to start yelling, but he never had the chance to yell. He stared at man cutting him and after a moment all that could be heard s a haunting breathy but quiet scream. No, there would be quick ending or bleeding out for man number ten. Walt spent just over an hour using his butterknives as scalpels. Each cut caused squirming and pain. The first cut was the cervical spine; the man couldn't move, but he could l feel what was happening. *That Walt* would take time to cut completely through his Achilles tendons, then between the toes. The man's eyes said everything that his body could not. Over that next hour, the young man endured more pain than *That Walt had* ever inflicted upon another human. By the end, the Walt side felt a bit sick, but *That Walt* pushed through the job. He always pushed through to finish the job. Always the trooper that he was.   He could

have made it last longer, but the young man was in

shock and just about dead when he ended it. He stood

and looked around the room: there was a lot of blood,

and no one was alive. As he left, he collected all the

knives which he used.

When he walked downstairs, it looked like he'd

missed q u i te the event. The frying pan guys had

indeed woken up and tried to escape. Ever the

perfectionist, *That Walt* had made extremely durable

knots. All of those men were no longer with us; he

thought and smiled. One last look around the living

room, it would likely appear another gang had done

this. Walt had taken the knives and pans into the

kitchen and washed them. Two reasons for that:

removing fingerprints and blood. If the police even

came into the kitchen, they wouldn't look through the

dishes. But being thorough had always been one of the

things that made *That Walt* dangerous.

He gave himself a once over to see if he had been cut, scratched, or damaged in any way. These poor gangbangers, idiots that they were, were dangerous only with guns in their hands or in numbers. Walt hadn't imagined that it would be difficult, but the relative ease had been surprising.

He was driving home when the body soreness first hit him. He was achy from kicks and punches thrown, and he thought to himself that he'd always been, and would continue to be, a dangerous man. But he was right, that side of him would never return. His body was too old, and this mission had taken every bit of rage from him. It was a strange drive home; no bit of rage lingered anywhere inside of him. Walt finally thought to himself, I can grieve.

Once Walt got home, the loneliness hit him. The house was empty, and utter loneliness hung in the air from the moment the door opened. He stared around the house. He was going to have to move. Yeah, the neighborhood would be safe for now. But the people that he knew here were gone. Maybe he would move closer to the ocean; his therapist had told him that ocean sounds were soothing.

That was all for the future. Tonight, he would celebrate his revenge. He walked into the study, his safe space. His body was in absolute pain as he got into his chair. He looked around at the books. His mind thought of each man that he had killed tonight, each detail of each life that he had ended. He leaned all the way back and placed his arms on the armrests.

Then he began to weep. This time, he held nothing back. He'd gotten his revenge, but what no one ever tells you is that revenge can never change what happened or bring back what you lost. Revenge is a falsity. There is nothing that cures loss, sadness, or pain.

As he slept, he dreamed of an afternoon spent at the beach with Nancy and Benny. It had been sometime that past summer. And he rested well.

The Waning Moments of Mitch

Mitch: I just stood there as she walked away. I couldn't say or do a thing. I was frozen in that moment for what seemed like an eternity. "I just can't be with a soldier," she had said.

Mitch: That was the last sentence that she ever spoke to me. And she just continued walking. It doesn't hurt as much—I guess it wasn't me, it was the life that I had chosen. I am a soldier. I am what I had chosen to be. Maybe not what I was ever meant to be, but here I was.

Mitch: Alone. Loneliness gets easier, you learn to drink it away. To throw yourself into what you do. You become cold, bitter, and ready to kill. That was what she didn't like. I had become this mean drunken person that she no longer recognized.

Mitch: So many years now, I'm still alone. Being a soldier is good for passport stamps, but not so much for having a family. So, I frequent the dive bars in town, looking for people my age that want to swap stories about how much life sucks.

Mitch: Is it that bad for everyone? No, there is help out there, but maybe I don't want it. Maybe I'll find out that I'm broken as a person and all of it is just my fault. Once in the field, I heard a guy explain what happens when a soldier dies. I've never forgotten that.

Mitch: A soldier is facing his imminent demise. The would-be killer begins to taunt him; tells him he wants to put the fear of God into him before he finishes him. The soldier begins to laugh. At first quietly, then a guffaw. The would-be saboteur asks him, "Why are you fucking laughing, idiot?" The soldier replies, "I don't fear God or man. Man can only hurt you till you die. And God? Well, God wants nothing to do with me." So, the man kills the soldier.

Mitch: As the soldier walks through a haze, he sees a man waiting for him. He asks, "Where am I?" The man says, "You're in heaven." Confused, the soldier says, "What'd I do to get here?" The man says, "Follow me." As they walk, he explains, "You see, all soldiers come here. It's their sacrifice and willingness to die for others that earns them a seat at this table. Ah, here we are!" The man says this quite happily.

Mitch: "Okay, where is here?" The guide answers, "My dear boy, this is the soldiers' section, your friends are waiting."

Mitch: "Your friends are waiting." That's the part I've never forgotten. At least I'll have friends somewhere.

The nurse smiled at Mitch as he floated off to sleep, alone. He'd not had any family other than the military all his adult life. This nurse, Nancy, that had looked in on him over the last couple of years was the closest thing he had to a friend or family. In the last few days of his life, he repeated that story to her about twenty times, and Nancy had paid attention each time. She felt that he had earned that much after thirty years in the military. He'd given it all to the military and it left him utterly alone in his final days.

Mid-shift this evening, Mitch found his way to

the Soldier's Section that he had been talking about,
Nancy was not present. He went the way he came into
the world—alone.

She ended her shift and hopped in her car,
ready to see her husband and children. It had been a
long day. She had considered the old man a friend.
She wept quietly in her car on the ride home.

She parked and began to walk into her home. It
began to snow.

Lonely are the Dead

He rises with the sun each day; he walks about the gardens of stone and moss. Each day flows into the next, with no real sense of meaning. The smell of the flowers is what he misses the most on the foggy mornings. Atticus has been a caretaker, of sorts, for as long as he'd care to remember. Anderson Hall is centuries old, and the attached cemetery is just as old.

As the caretaker, he assures that everything stays moving smoothly. The mourning are comforted. Everyone knows what to expect next. You could say Atticus is not only in charge, but a people person.

Atticus has only one issue. When he died over three hundred years ago as the Lord of Anderson Hall, he was the first laid to rest in the recently consecrated cemetery. What the living don't know is that the first individual laid to rest remains to help others cross over to their eternal life.

The first fifty years were strange. Family came one after the other. His wife and children; it was difficult when they arrived, as he could only see them. The guide's job is only to point them to where they must go. There is no light, no tunnel, no God waiting for them. Instead, they go to exist on a different plane. The other downside of being a guide is that the souls he guides only see an apparition with no real definition. He couldn't tell his wife how much he missed her, tell his children how beautiful and handsome they had grown to become. He was an apparition with a finger to point them to their next stop.

There were no instructions for Atticus. In fact, no retaker ever received instructions. They just *knew* what to Early on, when distant relatives and the people of the age were buried, it wasn't a difficult task. It was like being dropped into water as a baby;

you start to swim after a moment.

Now, centuries later, still in the shadow of Anderson Hall, Atticus is beginning to wonder, "When does it end? Will it end?"

"I'm tired," he speaks into the ether. But he doesn't know if it will end. Is this his penance for being the first in the ground? Not having a soul to speak to, hold, or cry with. He wonders how much longer he can send souls into the abyss beyond the cemetery—far beyond his purview. When will it be his time? In limbo, there are no tears. So, he struggles with the indeterminable sadness that engulfs him.

Through the years he's learned the limits of his work. He can only skirt the length and width of the cemetery. He has never been heard nor seen by a living person since his death. The ones that he guides seem to only see him as vapor. They don't really acknowledge him in any way. The newly dead just follow the general directions given by the hazy figure that is Atticus. Deep down, though, he knows he's not *"the Death,"* he's merely an extension of the famed hooded, scythe carrying main man. Are there restless souls the world over doing Death's dirty work? Why can't he just do it himself?

Still, the question that he ponders between the funerals and the moments of leading the dead, and the infernal sadness of being so alone-- when will he rest?

Is there no way for the dead to die? He's not a physical body—the tiresome part of his existence is merely existing. It's like being a child waiting for Christmas. You grow so tired of waiting and it never seems to get any closer. At least, Christmas arrives for children. Will his Christmas ever arrive? The moments trickle by like wet sand in an hourglass. His truth? That no matter the loneliness, anger, and solitude he feels; Atticus wouldn't want to wish this existence on anyone or anything else.

The minutes, the hours, the days, all flow into the centuries; to Atticus, it may well have been millennia that he had merely existed. *How does a dead man still feel such desperation? H*e thinks to himself. *Why can't I just rest?*

There will be a funeral soon, he senses the men preparing a new grave; he feels another soul to guide will arrive soon. He only sees them once they are covered with the cemetery's soil. He doesn't recognize the names or the people any longer. Anyone he ever knew has been gone for hundreds of years. So, he points, and they go, points, and they go. It's what he's done for longer than he cares to remember.

Everything beyond the limits of the cemetery is hazy, then the men arrive preparing the ground. They look so different: the clothes the men wear, their hair. All so different.

The chairs, a canopy, and the funeral is set. Atticus awaits the funeral's end. Once the dirt hits the coffin, he'll see the next spirit to guide.

And like a flame from a fire, he sees him rise. A young man, maybe in his twenties, is rising into the air. In that moment, Atticus feels strange, as he doesn't know where to guide him. Every time before, his arm would rise and simply point to where the spirit needed to go. After so many times, it was the arm just moving that continued to astound him.

His arms to his sides; Atticus stares as the young

man comes into view and stares directly at him. Atticus is shaken for a moment and then is thrown for a loop when he hears, "Hello. Where am I?"

Atticus, in shock, says nothing. He merely stares in disbelief. Could this person be talking to him?

"Sir, I'm David Simmons. Do you know where I am?"

With no throat to clear, Atticus finally speaks up. "You died. I… I'm sorry. I'm here to guide you to wherever you go next on your journey."

"I died? But h—Oh my God! It was a car accident!" David looked sad and then looked directly at Atticus, "How long have I been dead?"

"I don't know. I've been here for a while, but I can't see beyond the limits of this cemetery. How can you see me?"

"What?" David is trying to gather his thoughts

then speaks to Atticus, "I mean, you just appeared, bud."

Atticus thinks that David is remarkably calm for someone that just stepped into a new existence.

"Bud? No, my name is Atticus. Please, David, tell me, what year is it?" Atticus wearily asks.

It has been so long since he was able to communicate with anything or anyone that he feels queasy once he hears the answer.

"2025. July 2025. Why?" David responds calmly. "Why, Atticus?"

As David tries to focus on Atticus, the other specter is beginning to shrink away from David. He has a distraught look fall upon his face, "David, I died in 1658. The last person I spoke to was my wife." The two men float along, side by side. "And that was before I died. I knew it was a long while, but knowing the year is rather devastating. I'm sorry, I wasn't as ready to hear that as I thought I might be."

"1658? You're joking, right?" David is surprised. "But wait. How can you guide them if you can't speak to them?"

Still, Atticus is lost in thought. How long is that? Nearly four hundred years? Four hundred years. How many lifetimes is that? Are there any more people related to him still alive? Having heard that reality was harsh.

"David, I'm going to need a minute. I'll explain what I know, but please give me a moment."

Atticus moves away from David to think. He would have wept if he were able. It is surreal, for in the moments after, he stares into the distance, the green hills of what has become his realm. The more people buried, the more he can see. Confusion and sadness, it's all he can feel. When he finally comes to himself, he looks at David and he's ready to speak.

"David, is the land still owned by the Anderson family? Does Anderson Hall still stand?" He needs to know if it's still his family's land.

"Oh, yes, Anderson Hall is still here. But uhhh, the cemetery belongs to the community now. I mean, I'm not an Anderson. They bury everyone in the community here."

Atticus is confused. "The community? How large is the community, and what is this place called now?"

"It's called Bridge City. Anderson Hall is a tourist attraction. People from all over come to visit it." David speaks slowly, as if Atticus is a child.

"Tourist? What are those?" Atticus feels like a child learning new words.

"They're people that come to walk through the home to look at it. It's really old." Catching the look from Atticus, David pauses, "I mean, it's been here for a very long time. We would visit here when I was a kid, it was a school trip."

"Do any Andersons still live, David?" Atticus has finally come to the question that burns brightest in his mind.

"Not that I know of Atticus, I'm sorry," David says to the sad man that stands across from him.

"My family's name ended? When did it happen, do you think? Other than a building and a garden for the dead. That is a sad ending, is it not, David?" Atticus moves away slowly.

Atticus wondered to himself, when had he led his last relative to rest? When had his line ended?

"Atticus, how long will I be here with you?"

David is attempting to get his new friend's attention away from his new reality. "Atticus?"

"Yes, David. I… I don't know when you will be going. You're the first person I've been able to directly communicate with since starting this *job*. I just see a spirit and either my right or left arm rises and points them to where they will go. I've never known where they are going. I just point and then in moments, I'm alone again."

The two men are at rest and speak of time and change, of things that David knows of that had happened during his life. Atticus learns of cars, the internet, mothers that work, burritos, and so many things that are confusing but curious at the same time.

For every new thing that David introduces, it seems that Atticus introduces aspects of what he did.

It's boring. Atticus relays to David that he doesn't know why he was chosen, when he will leave, or what the totality of his mission might be here. Two or three funerals come and go; David watches as Atticus becomes translucent and quiet, his arm rises, and the new person floats away.

"Tell me, Atticus, do you thin—" The dead stop of the question is felt by both men.

Atticus stares back. "I felt it too, David. There's a shift."

"A shift? What does it mean?"

"David, this is new. I don't know what means."

As the days flowed into weeks, the two men continued to speak, gleaning from one another bits of their lives. They had become friends, but Atticus sees it begin to happen as it always did when they were led away. David is fading.

Atticus is starting to imagine another few centuries alone. Hundreds of years, floating about with no one to share feelings, thoughts, or memories with. It is strange; for as long as he's been dead, Atticus still remembers every detail of his living life. His wife, children, his family. And he also remembers his time alone, the centuries, and dreads that it is starting again. And he sadly thinks to himself, "It's a shame that the dead can't cry."

When he'd been six years old, he fell and injured his left arm. His mother had patched him up; she comforted him by singing him a song that she would sing to him whenever he'd get hurt. He hadn't grown up at Anderson Hall; his father Benjamin was a self-made man that came into means by way of owning fields of sugar cane. He would buy the land that would find the beautiful Anderson Hall sitting upon it. Benjamin had died years ago, but the time of his passing he was sent to his own father's land for burial. So, Atticus' mother had lived in Anderson Hall alone for a long while. Atticus had built a business in the shipping trade. While he travelled the sea, his wife and children stayed with his mother at Anderson Hall. After only a few years, Atticus made his money and then decided to stay home with his family. He'd found good men to continue his company. Unknown to him, he only had two more years to live once he stopped working. In a bit of irony, it was Atticus himself that had created the cemetery when his mother fell ill in the winter after his family had all moved in together at Anderson Hall. In the grand scheme of things, Atticus felt that forty years was a short life, but he didn't have a choice.

Atticus had fallen ill from his years on the sea, developing a lung disorder. During his time of existence, his illness could not have been prevented.

David hears Atticus tell him about what had caused his death. He keeps his opinion to himself, but it sounds like a case of pneumonia. Even early in the twentieth century, Atticus would have survived. It's sad to even imagine how poor medicine was so long ago. The two men speak of so many things, while talking is still available. As the days pass, David quietly grows worried, as Atticus is visibly fading. The scary part for both is that their voices have begun to sound distant. David and Atticus know that their time together is ending.

Atticus is sad. He will soon be alone again. In the sadness that has come to engulf his heart, he is reminded of his mother's singing…

"Look up, my son, our time has come to be at peace. Look up, my son, your pain is now at ease. So, please… sit in my arms. Mother is here to hold you for the rest of time. You'll

be better, you will see, things will be... Lean into me and look

into my eyes. We'll have blue skies..."

The song had gotten him through so many pains as a child. He had changed it for his own children, but it always warmed his heart to sing it. His wife and children had survived him. With all of his heart, he wanted to find them, to see them, and hold them close. For what reason had he been stuck here alone for so long. Alone. And David had said nothing to him, but Atticus knew that familiar aesthetic of the hazy floating being. David would soon be gone.

It's interesting, he's never actually tired. He cannot sit or lie down, he doesn't sleep. As a dead man, a guide for the other dead, the only thing he has ever felt during his time here is lonely.

Atticus stares toward the sun. It's beginning to set, another night in the cemetery. Another night in the middle of eternity; it doesn't matter when it started. He's only sure that it will never end.

Then, it happens. In an instant, something changes. Something new. And something new can't be bad, can it? For the first time in all his time in this purgatory, there's a different thing happening. What had been clear was now becoming hazy and distant. He knows it's time to say goodbye to David. It was back to being alone. Back to the eternal purgatory that was the bane of his existence.

"David, where are you?" Atticus is scared because this new thing has become scary. In these centuries of guiding people to their next phase, he'd only had the one friend: David. So, the entire process felt different, but familiar. A hazy David would soon lead to loneliness.

But it's more different than he thought; he sees

David in the distance. He knows it's David, but he can no longer see him. David is ethereal, and Atticus finally sees what he has shown hundreds of others. David is the one pointing. As clear as a moonlit night, David is pointing to the right.

Atticus knows what to do. He looks to his right and begins to move. It's beautiful. There is a light, but it's not the sun. This is the place where his family is waiting; he knows this like he knew the face of his father. His wife and children (grown men now) and his parents are waiting for him. The centuries have all melted away and they are together again.

Atticus quickly forgot about Anderson Hall, the time spent in the cemetery as Death's sidekick, and, lastly, David. He's home. For all he knows, everyone has their own paradise, and a simple truth is that everyone sees what they want to see in their personal paradise. It doesn't matter to him if these people are just his memories. They are going to be together, and that's all that matters.

As David's arm comes down, he realizes that he doesn't even remember bringing it up into the air, and he becomes aware of the few things that have just happened. He has taken Atticus' job. He will be here now; he is sending people away. And he's going to be completely alone. His new reality has begun, and he knows only one thing; an eternity is how long he may be here, and he wonders, "Why me?"

He rises with the sun each day; he walks about the gardens of stone and moss...

Do It for Uncle Sam

Randy had no direction when heading into the last few months of high school. Sure, he was going to graduate (keeping your head down makes you look better to the teachers), but the charity of the educators in his school had gotten him through it all. College was not in the cards. He thought that maybe he could just jump into the workforce.

The job search was slow, but it was going. His parents were talking to him about what his plans were and how he could not stay there for much longer after graduation. Basically, they told him to get ready to leave. It was a blow to him. He understood though; there were five more mouths to feed growing up in the house.

Living in a city, it might be easy to find a job. But the apartments are more expensive. Randy didn't have a car to get to a job, and even if he could get those two things together, he would not be able to afford a place to live.

He felt like it was all just fucked. Randy, from time to time, had dealt with anger. Being forced to leave made him feel belittled and frustrated. For all the outside world had known, he was a quiet and unassuming kid that sat quietly in school and did what he could to stay under the radar. In his mind, Randy was paranoid and anxious about what was ahead of him.

Randy didn't realize how truly strange his personal thoughts were. He had always thought about those things. The way that things ended; in those last moments, he knew that maybe something had been wrong with him all the time. It's a strange thing, the fleeting moments before your death; how clear things become. His paranoia was just that. None of it had ever been real. The clarity of the end. It brought tears to his eyes, but on this day so many years earlier, he had thought he was an average guy.

As the days passed by, he was feeling the pressure build. What would he do? It was the week before spring break when all the seniors were sent to the school's testing center. There were several soldiers at the front of the classroom. They spoke about the military. How today's military was the best in the world, and they needed people like the ones in this room. Afterward, all the students were given the opportunity to take a military aptitude test named the ASVAB.

Randy didn't think twice about it. Maybe he could join the military. He'd never thought about joining before, but some plans were better than no plans. So, he stayed, took the test over the next several hours, and then waited to hear about the results. The Army recruiter had been the first person to contact him within a week. It was a phone call on their home phone—Randy's parents couldn't afford a cellphone for any of their children. His mother had answered and asked who was calling.

"Randy, a Sergeant Anderson from the Army is calling you. Randy?" she yelled in a bit of confusion.

"I'm coming, Mom." *That was quick*, he thought to himself. He hoped it was good news. He picked up the receiver and whispered, "Thanks, Mom."

"What is this about?" His mother whispered to him.

Randy just smiled and held up a finger, asking for a moment. "Hello, Sergeant Anderson? Yes, this is Randy Tolliver."

"Hello, Randy. You recently took the ASVAB at your local high school. I'm your local Army recruiter. Do you have time to chat about your results and options?"

"Sure, where is your office? I don't have a car, but I can take a bus."

"Randy, I can come by and pick you up, then we can speak at my office. Would you be comfortable with that?" Sergeant Anderson was polite and well-spoken.

Randy said, "Yes, sir. That works for me."

"Just call me Sergeant. Anderson. And if address is the one on the ASVAB paperwork, I can be by in about fifteen minutes."

"Great, Sergeant Anderson, I'll be looking out. Thank you." Randy ended the call, hung up the receiver, and then spoke to his mother. "Mom, I took a test last week and the Army recruiter wants to talk to me."

Randy was rarely excited by anything, and this

was rather nice for his mother to see. "That's really nice, Randy. Do you think you would like the Army?" His mother knew a few things about her own son. First, he was a moody person and could have a short temper. Second, listening to and taking orders were often difficult for him.

"I really don't know, Mom. I have to do something, right?" Randy responded. "I want to get some shoes on. I'll be here in just a bit."

Randy's mother's eyes followed her son for a moment, then she sat and suddenly wished that she and her husband could continue supporting Randy after graduation. She and David, her husband, had looked long and hard, but there was no financial way to keep him in the home any longer. As an adult, he needed to continue on his own. She had cried many nights about this very thing. She didn't know if Randy would ever want to be in the Army, but with the way the world was, she would be afraid for him to be in combat.

Sgt. Anderson picked up Randy, and they headed to the recruitment center. They sat down and spoke for an hour or so. Randy had done well enough on the ASVAB to join the Army. He was shown a list of jobs and was told he could ask anything he wanted about the descriptions. Randy saw a lot of words describing the jobs. He understood some of it, but some of it was confusing. Trying not to look foolish (in turn, becoming foolish for not asking), he stared at several jobs and noticed one that said *Engineer*.

As far as Randy knew, engineers designed buildings like architects. He didn't want to stall the process; he wanted to have a career, in place to go after he graduated. That same afternoon, he chose to enlist. Sgt. Anderson seemed excited; Randy had turned eighteen the November before his high school graduation.

"We'll need some more paperwork. Your Social Security card, birth certificate, and your transcripts. We can request y o u r transcripts with no issue if you sign some paperwork today. Can you get the other things in the next few days?"

Randy would not know at the time, but the recruiter's job was made easy by lost souls like him. No, recruiters were not forcing kids to sign up or take advantage of them (Well, not outright, but there were white lies and stretches in the truth every now and then). But lost kids with no aim or purpose j u s t needed a pat on the back, a few free lunches, and then, gotcha!

They don't volunteer the ins and outs of what you might be getting into. They have numbers to meet. It's a performance-based gig, and to perform you have to get the bodies to basic training.

Randy was told to get in shape, and there were training sessions, offered by the recruiters, every weekend to get to know the recruiters and other local recruits. But he also had to work out on his own. That evening he had gone home and told his parents about the news.

David spoke up quickly.

"Randy, the Army? Son, that's a hard life. Did you really think that you needed to move so fast?"

"Dad, you told me I had to get out in two months! Two fucking months!! So, yes, I had to move that fast!" Randy, was near tears, screamed at his father then stormed out of the room.

The next two months moved quickly; Randy worked out daily and diligently worked on the exact things his recruiter had told him to work on to be ready. He wanted to excel at something, for once in his life. He didn't want to be what Sgt. Anderson called a "limp dick" Private, meaning the weak link, a burden to his squad, and a likely wash out when all was said and done. Randy would be headed to Fort Leonard Wood, Missouri, for his Basic Training. He'd never been out of the state of Washington, so there was an adventure ahead of him.

Basic Training was not physically difficult; he'd prepared well. But the mental aspect was a bit more difficult; actually, he was fighting his violent urges to explode. So far, he had hidden it very well, but Randy felt on edge most days. Lack of sleep and different instructions from different directions and different Drill Sergeants had made him feel confused and angry. Sgt. Anderson had warned him to be a listener and hard worker.

"Keep your ears open, mouth shut, and do what's asked of you! No more and no less. You don't have to be remembered by anyone," Randy recalled Sgt. Anderson telling him, "Concentrate on making yourself an outstanding soldier. Everything else is gravy."

Basic Training was ending, the soldiers were getting more sleep, and Randy was feeling more in control of his anger and emotions. He was one of the younger guys in his platoon; his family could not make the trip from Washington. After Basic Training graduation, Randy walked around aimlessly, staring at the other soldiers with their families. Hugs, laughs, and tears amongst the small groups that had formed. Randy felt a pang of sadness, but he tucked it away. He walked to a taxi stand and hopped in a cab.

Randy had gone to dinner at a local restaurant

by himself. Being quiet, hardworking, and no nonsense had, indeed, not made him popular. Even to the serious guys he seemed a bit tightly wounded. Too serious and angry. Behind his back, the other soldiers thought that he seemed like one of those dudes that would "climb a clocktower." They called him a "cheese eater" and a "try hard"; Randy made no friends, but no enemies either. He was invisible.

The guys left him alone, and Randy never even got that they were making fun of him when he did speak to anyone. He would be asked ridiculous questions, and he answered them in earnest—what Randy didn't ger was the sarcasm of the questions and his lack of awareness put a target on him. He thought that they may have looked up to him or didn't understand something that they had learned. When they laughed, Randy would laugh as well, but he didn't know why.

Their advanced training would begin the following Monday. So that Saturday night, while all the other soldiers spent time with family and friends that had come to watch them graduate, Randy spent the evening alone in the barracks reading about next week's training and what he had to look forward to.

It was probably two a.m. when Randy felt something touching his face. It was the flashlights and the laughter that woke him all the way up. It was an older guy, Ray Francis; he was a guy from upstate New York. Francis was also an instigator when it came to what he thought of as a practical joke. Randy moved back and sat bolt upright and discovered that Francis was rubbing his dick on the side of Randy's face. Randy leapt at him and never spoke a word.

In the interviews with military police and the chain of command the group of soldiers that had been there said that it was a joke that had just gone wrong. They had done their best but had not been able to stop Randy from beating PFC Francis to death.

Randy got up and was going to push the guy and yell at him, but it was Francis's grinning face that pushed him over top. He started beating the man with his left fist, five or six landing before a couple of soldiers attempted to grab him. Randy easily shook them off and went back to beating on Francis's face. At this point, Francis was sitting up, bloody but he was still alive.

Randy then thrust his left foot to Francis's sternum. At the hearing, the coroner would testify that this was what likely what had led to the death of PFC Francis. The force of the kick had cracked the man's sternum, but then Randy knelt on the cracked sternum; the force from the knee had sent shards of bone into the man's heart. Randy continued to punch the man that was struggling for air as his heart hemorrhaged blood.

Four soldiers were able to get Randy off Francis. Witnesses would say that the bloody man on the floor was dead, he was gurgling blood, but it was just the air being released from his body. Randy was held back and told to just sit down. PVT Green had run downstairs to the staff duty desk yelling for help. Two drill Sergeants had gone upstairs. Upon seeing Francis lying in a pool of blood, they knew that he was gone.

Drill Sgt. Edwards, a muscular black man, and very capable soldier had spoken first, "Private Tolliver. Stand up and walk with me."

Edwards had been Randy's platoon sergeant; he knew him well and trusted the drill sergeant. When Randy heard the voice, he snapped back to the current situation. This moment would matter and he would cooperate immediately.

As they got up, Drill Sgt. Edwards looked over to a soldier that had come up with them and spoke calmly, "Go call 911, tell we have one to for the hospital and one for the MP's."

Randy and Drill Sgt. Edwards sat downstairs in the common room, the doors were closed and the senior man in the room spoke, "Tolliver, I'm no MP, you know me. You've been in my platoon since day one. This is just me and you. I want you to tell me what happened?"

Reality set in, and Randy felt like he was finally back in his own skin, "I don't know, Drill Sgt. He put his dick on my face and they were laughing. Francis looked at me like I was some weak ass bitch. Fuck them all, they grabbed me from behind, I could have finished my job. I'm a soldier, Drill Sgt. I'm not weak anymore, and I will never be weak again."

Drill Sgt. Edwards simply stared at the young soldier,

Tolliver was a lost soul. Edwards had been on the trail for several cycles and soldiers like Tolliver came through very rarely. This boy was squared away on the outside—he did everything by the book, outworked everyone, went beyond what he could from time to time, but otherwise, he never brought attention to himself.

To the untrained eye, Randy was invisible. To a drill sergeant like Edwards, who was a combat veteran and had seen many soldiers through his career, the energy that came off of Tolliver was 100% crazy. Doing enough right, so that his scores on tests and readiness looked good, but not enough to draw attention to himself. Tolliver was full of hate and sadness that held no future and a madness that would have made him a great soldier—no fear or regret, just rage.

The Drill Sgt. knew that this would end up badly for Tolliver. He patted him on the shoulder and spoke softly about staying calm, being honest and direct when the MPs arrived.

"Tolliver, you did what any man would do. Killing is a

soldier's work. You did what we trained you to do."

Drill Sgt. Edwards walked away and left him alone in the common room. As he made it to the staff parking lot, he took out a crumpled pack of Newports and took one out and lit up. He let the menthol hit his chest, rubbed his tired eyes and let out a cloud of smoke. "Fuck, man. Good soldier gone to waste."

Randy was arrested that night. No, the circumstances did not look good, but what Francis and his buddies had done would be of help in the trial. That, and some of the language in Randy's answers had led the military police to have him mentally evaluated.

"What did you mean that you had only seen black when were beating on PFC Francis? Was it dark or was it something else?"

Randy was confused for a moment. "It was dark, but after the first hit I just kept hitting. There was nothing there. I just couldn't stop."

"Okay, PVT Tolliver. I understand. Has that ever happened to you before? During your time in the Army or before?"

"Yes." Randy felt trapped and scared. He only wanted to tell the truth.

"Can you tell me about that?" The doctor sat back and just wanted to listen. He placed his pen and pad on the table to put Randy at ease.

"I got into a fight at a party when I was in high school. Some guy pushed me. So, I beat on him."

"Beat on him? How badly?"

"I don't know." Randy began rubbing his hands together as he thought about the fight, "I, uh, I beat on him till I got tired. He was a college guy; I don't know how it ended."

Randy was just speaking like the doctor was an

old friend. He felt nervous about what he was saying, but at least someone was listening to him.

"He just pushed you, PVT Tolliver?" The doctor did lean in to take a note.

"Yes, but he didn't say excuse me. I had just pissed in a bush, and he had walked into me. I stared at him for a moment, so he stopped turned around and said something like, 'What are you gonna do, bitch?' So, I just wailed. No one was around. I finally stopped when he wasn't moving."

"What happened after that?" More notes were taken.

"I breathed." Randy said the only thing that came to mind. The doctor nodded and wrote a few more notes.

There were a lot of questions, and Randy did his best to answer them. Francis had died on the barracks floor. He was taken to the post hospital where he was pronounced dead.

Randy didn't really understand everything that had happened, but he was separated from the Army and sentenced to time served, as he had been sitting there for about eight months waiting for his trial.

All that Randy was able to understand was that he was ruled not mentally competent on the night of the attack. They called it a psychotic snap. The deceased soldier had sexually assaulted Randy, per the court's statement, and that precipitated the attack that cost him his own life.

The other soldiers that had been there had stated that Francis was indeed rubbing his penis on Tolliver's face. It was just a joke that went too far. They just thought the quiet guy would take it, and it would be over. They never expected him to get that angry. The soldiers that had attempted to stop him stated that Tolliver was like an "animal" and far too "out of control" to stop.

"It took about six of us to get him off of Francis, and the way that he was laughing and crying was scary." That was the official statement given by PV2 Richard Sanders. In court, Randy had heard that account for the first time. He didn't remember laughing and crying, but then, he didn't say that he didn't remember any of it.

The prosecution, for their part, still wanted to get some jail time for Randy. So, they showed pictures of the damage done to Francis. Randy had not seen the results of what he had done before that moment. He looked away (it was what he should do), then realized in a small corner of his mind that he wanted to look at the pictures. He would hide the wide smile that his mind had created.

He didn't understand why he liked it so much.

He'd never felt that type of euphoria when it came to anything else, just violence. The last time that he beat on someone, the guy at the party, it wasn't like he told the doctor. The guy had bumped into him and did call him a bitch. But Randy had waited until the guy was headed toward his car. Randy followed him and made sure that they were alone. Then he sprang into action. "Hey."

The guy got the last couple of words out of his mouth that he would ever speak: "Yeah, what th—"

Just as Randy had told the doctor, he did beat the guy up and he did walk away unnoticed. Another thing that he left out was that he knew that man had died before he left. He knew how badly he had beaten him; he was always keenly aware when he had been violent. And Randy had a long-hidden history of violence.

In the city, you can hide a lot of things. There were a million faces in the crowd, and Randy was one that needed that. Hiding in plain sight was a gift when you were a killer. It was one person after another. He'd been able to function under the radar his entire life.

It started when he was seven. The young girl's name was Sandy. A couple of the boys at the pool had teased Randy because their names rhymed.

"Randy and Sandy sitting in a tree, k-i-s-s-i-n-g." And then they laughed very loudly.

It had made the girl cry. And Randy had never liked bullies. He waited for the boys to start swimming. It had looked like an accident; the boys were splashing water on one another when Randy had jumped onto both of them. The smaller of the boys ended up with a broken collarbone, and the other was not as lucky. Randy had hit the side of his head and knocked it right into the side of the pool.

The blood had been tremendous. Everyone had to get out of the pool. Sandy had left with her family. Randy wondered if she w a s impressed by his work. He hopped up, apologizing profusely to the boys. After his parents had pulled him out of the pool and apologized to the families for him, they left. When they got him to the car, they asked just what the hell he was thinking. Of course, Randy played dumb, said he was just playing. They never returned to the public pool again.

For every "accident" that he'd ever caused, there were plausible excuses. The guy in high school was the last time, before Francis, that he had killed. He knew the kid was dead. He had thrown him into the brush beside the road and left him there. It was a house party, very loud and lots of people from all over. Randy had disappeared into the night. It didn't bother him to hurt others. He didn't get emotional. Violence had always been a bit of fun for him. If it happened in front of others, though, needed to learn the proper human emotions. For someone like Randy, who some would call a sociopath. He had no science and just really didn't care. As a teenager, he had realized what was happening. He began watching people in public to understand them. How emotion should look and sound. Studying television programs and reading about human emotions. You need to know when to smile, look shocked or sad. The hardest part was pretending to cry during emotional moments. Over time, he would get better at it. That had been important when it came to the night Francis picked on him. He was laughing—well, it was funny—but as Francis was starting to bleed a lot, Randy saw tears coming from the dying soldiers' eyes. *Dammit, Randy, you made him cry*, he had thought to himself. So, the tears flowed, but he couldn't contain his laughter. Randy had never thought about it, but the combination of both made him sound more connected to emotions.

He snapped back to what was happening in the courtroom; it required respect and attention. So, he dug deep and found the definitions and tried to show them correctly. In end, after the Francis family yelled that it wasn't right, and he was waiting for a van to take him to the airport, one of Company drill sergeants, a large man that Randy had seen, walked by and stopped to speak with him. "Tolliver."

Randy went to pop up and yell, "*Yes, Drill Sergeant!*", but he was stopped by the man that had spoken to him.

"Sit down, Tolliver. You don't have to do that anymore." The hulking man sat next to him. "This is a shitty situation. We need every swinging dick that can hold a weapon and is willing to kill to be on the frontlines. And an asshole like Francis had to fuck it up for a guy like you. We all knew that you were a good soldier. You were squared away, and it looked like you had a bright future in this man's Army."

"Thank you." Randy spoke quietly.

"Yeah, guys like Francis, they fuck around and find out, right?" He finished with a laugh and stood to walk away. He stopped looked over his shoulder and added, "Goddamn, kid, that hand to hand combat class did you some good."

"I guess so." Randy let out an awkward laugh. But he was confused by how the conversation had ended. Was the drill sergeant just like him?

"Well, it's too bad, son. With rage like that, you

should still be in our Army. Hell, you should have had a nice long career. Killing someone is never easy. We should still have you in active duty, killing like that for Uncle Sam."

Randy was intrigued by what he had been told. Is it natural for someone to make it in the Army with sociopathic personalities? Maybe, maybe not. It took someone a bit different to yell about blood making grass grow or speaking about one shot, one kill. Randy had not felt anything either way, but it was enjoyable to yell about killing and blood. He had learned a lot about killing, fighting, and survival during Basic Training. But he never got to learn his job.

Eventually, when he was getting ready to arrive back in Washington, he realized that he had continued to call his parents and write to them but had never told them what had happened. So, it was time to lie.

He took a taxi home. He limped as he walked into the house and weaved a tale of how he had been hurt in training. He would only need to hang out for a week to get back on his feet. His parents bought it, told him he could use the couch (one of his siblings now owned his old room), and if it took more than a week, they understood.

He found a job one day later at a coffee processing warehouse. It was a bit south of the city, but he could take a couple buses and be there on time. He would have a good paycheck in two weeks. Once the check arrived, he said goodbye to his family. The next time they would hear about him would be on the last day of his life, almost a decade later.

There was a motel that had monthly rates, and he had enough to move in there. He lived cheaply, saving as much as he could. At nineteen, he was all alone. He didn't hang out with anyone from work, never contacted his family, nor did he seek any woman's company. In the next few years, he would hang onto that job, get a better place to live, and date a few times. It was purely the physical need to have sex; masturbation got boring after a while. He had no emotional connection with any one of those ladies. If one was particularly good in bed, he would find a way of digging deep to use those fake emotions for at least a while. Until he got bored. Then he moved on to the next.

He could go a long time without companionship. Randy found it easier to masturbate; he could go at a pace he liked, and when he was done, there was no one huffing and puffing in his face or trying to hold him. Being alone was easy.

It continued that way for about ten years. He really had grown bored of being "good," it had gotten to be too much. Too much of fighting the want to kill, to hurt or maim. He wanted to release the beast inside of him.

Randy started slowly, going to areas where there were a lot of homeless people. The sad reality of the homeless population is that a majority of people that have nice homes and warmth or air conditioning (depending on the season) do not care what happens to the people that live on the streets. Over several weeks, he had beaten several men and women to death. It had been a bit of a thrill (as much as Randy could identify with that feeling). When he heard about his work on the local evening news, he simply wanted to do it more. The power that he felt when a person was begging for him to stop.

Then, all in a moment, Randy woke up one morning and was tired of everything. Beating people, finding nice women to spend the night with, he'd even grown tired of masturbating. It all came together on a Thursday morning. He called in sick. It wasn't a big deal, because he was always there and on time. supervisor told him to feel better soon.

In a creepy way, Randy enjoyed his answer: "Oh, I'll feel better. Very soon."

He hung up the phone, then went online and requested all his bank accounts to be closed and had a cashier's check forwarded to parents' home. He spent about ten minutes writing down instructions for his parents.

He wanted to be cremated and just thrown away; nowhere that anyone could find him. Randy then thought for a moment and wrote a letter that would help his parents with questions that might arise.

"Mom and Dad,

My life was a mix of trying to be good and failing, and just existing. Don't blame yourselves or my environment; if anything, the two of you did your best and any child in that home was set up to do better than they had started. I simply have no feelings of fear, sadness, hate, or empathy. I'm empty inside and that is just chemicals. I was never bothered that I had to leave, money is money and you didn't have that much. I do hope that what I am sending to you all is of help. I think that the public will try to make this about you. No one creates a sociopath; I was born this way. No one could predict what I would do because each day was a choice, no forethought or consideration for consequence. As much as I can understand an apology, I give you that. As much as I am just a creature that kills at will and never knew how to care or love, I can say that you deserved better from a son.

Thank you—

Randy"

Randy knew that they would hear about why he had left the Army, at least the real reason. How experts would come forward with their take on the man that had been their son. How the individual was probably never able to understand human emotion, that he had likely always felt disconnected. For all of a month, but likely much less, Randy Tolliver would be the poster child for mental illness and violence.

Randy ended the note with a signature. He didn't think that it was important to end it with "*I love you.*" He had never loved anything in his lonely and miserable life. He placed the letter in an envelope, sealed it, and placed a stamp on it. As he was leaving his place, he dropped the letter in the community mailboxes. Dropping the letter in the mailbox, in his mind, meant that there would be no turning back. The plan was in motion.

Randy drove to his local police station and pulled a weapon from under his seat. He popped the magazine out, checked it for ammunition, and slapped it right back in. The thing about small-town jails is that they don't typically have metal detectors. He walked in and, true to form, there was no beeping from a metal detector. So, he stepped to the front counter. He had to be careful about what he said, this would determine how the next few minutes p l a yed out.

"Hello, my name is Randy Tolliver. Do you have a detective on site that I can speak to about some of those killings in Seattle?", he sounded shy and boyish—a far cry from the man that stood before the dispatcher attached to the front desk.

The front desk officer looked at the man in front of him and politely answered, "Yes, sir. Please have seat. I'll have a detective up here in a couple of minutes."

Randy faked a smile and replied, "Thank you." He turned and found a chair and sat down to wait.

A woman, Detective Erin Davis, stepped out and looked about the empty lobby like there was a crowd. Her eyes settled on Randy, then she called for him, "Mr. Tolliver?"

"Yes, right here." Randy stood up and looked at the detective. He took a breath. He thought that talking loudly would bring the attention of the other officers. This was the next point of no return. With the letter already mailed to his family. He took two steps toward the detective, Detective Davis saw a calm, unassuming young man step toward her. No sense of danger ever occurred to her. Then he spoke.

"It was me. I beat those people to death!" He tried to sound emotional; he was trying to find the emotion of sadness. "You need to fucking arrest me right now."

Detective Davis took a step forward; the calmness of the man betrayed her own training and thoughts. Her guard was still down, and Randy could see that she meant to just talk.

"Look, sir, please relax. Now what's going on today? Let's go talk."

She was too calm; time to ramp it up. "I didn't come to talk to you, bitch. I came to bring the world pain!"

And it was time to ice the cake. He pulled out his gun and waved it around up in the air for a moment. He needed to give the detective time to get officers to back her up. She needed to get her weapon unholstered. Randy was facing her yelling about a lot of nonsense, not aiming yet. Just a few more moments, he thought.

He felt silly about just waving the weapon around. Still not directly at the detective, so as to make her feel comfortable enough to find cover and wait for her back up. Randy actually walked in a circle; that was cringy enough on its own, but he thought he couldn't keep this up.

At that moment, Randy heard footsteps behind him, and he knew the last step was almost here. Detective Davis had drawn her gun, but the barrel was pointed toward the ground. It was a safe position in case it went off. It was time…

The next few moments would be burned into

Erin Davis's mind for a very long time. She was an only child, single, and had been dating a guy that was an officer one town over. Erin had become a detective very early in her career, a fast tracker, and she worked very hard. Unlike TV shows, Erin found that real police officers rarely used their guns in the line of duty.

Ending the sad life of Randy Tolliver would be her first time having to use her weapon in the line of duty and the first time that she would end a life.

Randy turned his back on Detective Davis for a moment, long enough to look out of control; Still yelling, he'd added talking about killing a room full of pigs. Then came the moment. That moment he had arrived to get done. He spun about quickly and leveled the weapon at Detective Davis. She training kicked in, the barrel shot up toward the man, and she fired a round into his chest. He fell, and the weapon fell from his hand as he landed. Randy felt like he'd been hit by a truck, and it burned. He was coughing blood. He heard steps running toward him and then felt the thud of an officer kicking the gun away from him and his hand.

Detective Davis did her job by trying to calm him. But she quickly noticed he wasn't in any type of emotional anguish; the man seemed to be smiling as he coughed.

"Mr. Tolliver, we're calling an ambulance right now. We're going to save you; do you understand me?"

Randy spit out a mouthful of blood and spoke clearly. "Don't bother saving me, you did your job. I'm a killer," more blood pooled in his mouth, so he spit again, "I have always been this. Detective you did a good thing today."

Detective Davis had aimed center mass, it was aimed a bit to the right, she tried to avoid the left side of his chest; he had a chance of making it. By the book, Randy lay on the ground and squinted a bit, gathering a thought.

In his last coherent act, Randy paused to spit a last time so that his words would be clear:

"Sorry, I didn't choose you, you just came out. I'm not worth saving, just let me end…" He could no longer spit the blood out, so the final sentences were gurgled and hard to understand, "Please. The only thing I was ever good at was killing. I should have been smart and kept getting paid by Uncle Sam to do it. You know?"

Now his breathing was labored, but he was strangely calm. Randy then let out his last breath, and as he did, he smiled. His eyes stayed open, and Detective Davis just stared for a moment. She didn't touch him; she stood up and went to recover his gun. She knew immediately something was not right.

When Randy had popped the magazine out of the weapon, it was simply to ensure that it was indeed empty. He had never really liked guns. He was a more personal type of killer. Hands on.

Detective Davis popped the clip out, and her suspicions were correct. The man had walked into the police station with an empty gun so that the next detective on the walk-in roster could kill him; the popular term for what Randy had done was "Suicide by a police officer." *Son of a bitch*, she thought.

She looked down at the smiling dead man, wondering why he had done this and what he had been through. As Randy had predicted, his name was everywhere for the next few weeks. The man that had terrorized the homeless population, had killed a fellow soldier and was kicked out of the Army, the man that existed in the light of day by just staying quiet. A vicious serial killer with a multitude of bodies that he had left littering the Pacific Northwest.

For his part, Randy's smile had been the first real smile of his life. He had never felt emotion. It was strange to feel the euphoria of death. He could not have gotten that from taking his own life. That simple smile was his last conscious action.

He heard Drill Sgt. Edwards' words echoing in his head.

"You did what we trained you to do." Randy realized that his entire life was an attempt to feel, to belong, to exist, to be a human. He had failed at doing that, but as a killer—he had been a success. As the said in training when you completed a task, you were either a "go" or "no go."

Killing for Uncle Sam was all he was meant to do. Drill Sgt. Edwards and the other drill sergeants wanted success for him. He was a weapon. Nothing more or less. Never quite human. His breathing was no longer labored; his sad life was almost over. The blare of the ambulance in the distance signaled that they had almost arrived, but they were too late. In the darkness of what was left in him, Randy found no peace or answers. A life ending was not a brilliant event filled with stars and lights with tunnels; it was a man lying on the floor in a pool of blood, the smell of gun powder and the sickening smell of blood made everyone feel sick. The officers left the body alone in the lobby, Davis held the empty weapon that Randy had brought into the station. It was over. Mission accomplished, now he could rest.

The Collector

"Did his eye just make that popping sound?"

Pete giggled a bit, but responded, "At least fifty times I've stomped on a man's head and never have I heard a pop like that! Jesus Christ!!"

"Let's move, Pete. I'm seeing Sandy later."

The man, with only one eye remaining, lay on the floor whimpering. Still alive, he thought that he was going to leave there that night. Sure, a patch would be embarrassing, but at least he was alive. The two men with both eyes walked toward the apartment door.

"Look, we don't like fucking stomping on your head, do you understand that?"

Gathering himself, the man on the floor responded quietly, "Yeah…yeah, I'm sorry, guys. I won't ever skim again. The King's money is his money. I promise you; it won't happen again."

Jamie stopped short of the door and patted Pete on the back, saying something quietly, and Pete nodded and walked out. As Jamie turned, he looked down on the man lying on the floor and spoke in a calm manner.

"You're right. The King's money is just his. And he has never appreciated anyone skimming… Isn't that what you said? Skimming?"

"Yes, I sold his stuff, and I'll get all of his money to him."

"Funny thing, David. The King, in the end, doesn't care about money." Jamie took two steps toward a chair and sat. "The King values loyalty and respect a lot more than any amount of money."

"What can I do, sir?" The man on the floor was trying to stop his bleeding with his shirt, and attempting, in earnest, to stay alive. "I've got the

King's money, and I have a lot more in a safe. It's all his… All of it!"

Jamie gave his watch a look and knew his date was coming up and the cat and mouse game had run its course. "It's not money, now, is it?"

Suddenly the man on the floor realized two things. He could stop worrying about stopping his bleeding, and he was not ending the night alive. Still, he would ask for his life to be ended quickly. The King's worker could give him that much. As a thief, he wasn't really owed that quick death from The King's employees; the regretful thief knew that as an inexcusable truth.

In dealing drugs, you had to remember that a multitude of things can get you killed very quickly. But a way to keep yourself alive was honesty. David had known that the day that he approached a known dealer, and a man he considered a friend; asking how he could get started in the game. Two years later, he ran a section of the city for the King. Another two years passed and to people outside the game, he was a big shot. He always had blow, money, and beautiful women hanging around.

During the last few moments of his life, David thought of just how much time was wasted trying to look important, rich, and cool. It was all fake, but what he had done, he broke the rule. David had stolen from his supplier. He had not been honest.

The people outside of this office would hear the screams of pain, for however long the two men that came in to meet him tonight, would make it last. It was a message. A very clear message, you steal at your own peril.

No matter how David begged, Jamie couldn't give him the one request he had repeatedly made.

The death would be slow and painful, but a few minutes would be taken off due to Jamie's date.

David's sad end started with him getting his knees and lower legs broken with collapsible nightsticks. The men carried these to quickly disable their customer from running. It sounded painful, the screaming started immediately; The King's message was always clear— "Fuck with him at your own peril!" A few minutes in, Jamie took a break to get a drag from his vape (grape flavor), paused, and took a blade from a holder under his jacket. He had taken slices out of David that had left him in ribbons. The broken bones, nor his missing eye had caused his death. No, David lay there for another couple of hours, bleeding out from all of the cuts that Jamie had made. The two men walked out, closed the door, and looked about the club making sure that they caught eyes with everyone. It was their way of saying, we've seen you and we know that you will stay quiet. They told one of the bouncers to make sure no one opened that door tonight. As David lay there bleeding, he couldn't yell out. Jamie had taken an offering for the King.

Jamie had learned on their first night together, were it anything more than a message, that the King always asked for the tongue of someone that had betrayed him. What Jamie and Pete would always carry with them, when they made that last visit with someone, was a mouthguard case to carry that offering.

Jamie looked down at the one-eyed man as he lay there dying. It was the same thing every time: the person lay there bleeding out, a far-off look on their face as they faded away. The first five or ten times it had laid heavily on Jamie's shoulders. It took a certain kind of person to do this type of work.

Interestingly, you never know if you will be able to take a life until you have done it.

Sandy looked stunning, as usual. Jamie felt lucky to have met this smart, beautiful woman. She knew that he worked as a collector, and that was all that Jamie wanted to share. He felt that, should it come to it with Sandy, he would try to find a new job.

"So, how was your week, Sandy?"

"Not bad, couldn't wait for this dinner." She threw her hair over her shoulder, the smell when she did that drove Jamie wild. She used some type of natural fruity shampoo. That had been one of the first things that drew Jamie to her in that coffee shop.

It was rare that Jamie went to coffee shops, but that morning he'd been out of espresso at his place.

Such a long night always required loads of caffeine, and he had none. Who knew that he would meet the woman of his dreams there and that she wouldn't be some stuck-up psycho that typically hung out in those places.

He got behind her in line. He wanted to speak to her but thought to himself that no one would come to a coffee shop to be hit on. But something about this woman...

"Hi, I'm Jamie. Would you like to share a cup of coffee with me?" *Go big or go home*, he thought as he spoke.

"Well, aren't we brave. Jamie, is it?" she said with a grin.

"Bravery is a virtue too many have let go. I believe that you have to take your shot when you've got it."

In that moment he saw her smile, just for him, for the first time. He knew if she said yes to that coffee, he would work to stay with her for as long as she stayed with him. Jamie had never had a girlfriend, per se. Sure, he'd been with women since he was a teenager. But to want to just be with one person; that had never happened to him.

"You know what, why not. Hi, I'm Sandy."

"Okay, Sandy. What would you like to drink this fine morning?"

"I was just here for an espresso. I needed a bit of energy this morning."

He laughed and thought to himself that it was meant to be.

"And what's so funny about an espresso?"

"Energy is the only reason I came here today. I've never been here before."

They ended up sitting for several hours. They had more in common than Jamie ever thought they would have. She was a freelance writer and could sit at her leisure, so their visit was a nice one. It was another first for him, thinking of the word love as he looked at the woman that sat across from him.

Jamie had always thought of love at first sight as a thing from sappy rom coms, but here he was staring at Sandy with all thoughts of spending as much time with this woman as time would allow. What was different about her? Why today? It all seemed too well-planned. When everything lines up like dominoes about to make you say *Wow* as they fall into a beautiful pattern, it becomes apparent that you are just along for the ride.

You either become the domino that falls and misses its mark, or you make it to the end and you look back on the entire journey and the beautiful path that brought you there. All this went through his mind and a conversation happened on that day. Interestingly, he knew that Sandy felt the same way. He saw it in her eyes and felt it in her body language. So, he asked her to dinner, and six months later, they saw one another as often as possible.

It sounded like bad comedy. "The Writer and the Hit Man; brought to you by Preparation-H!" But it was a journey being together. Neither of them had broached being in a serious relationship before this. They were getting very close; he was surprised that he had no apprehensions. Life was very simple with Sandy. They didn't agree on everything but knew that it w a s all right to have your opinions. Two people can't agree on everything. If they do, then one of them has given up on themselves completely.

All the time with Sandy, she never knew. Sure, in

a city this size, he could stay there and no one would ever see him that had ever been the subject of a job for the King. Still, living here after leaving that life would make some things sketchy, at best. So, once it ended, he would speak to Sandy a b o ut stepping up their relationship, moving forward, and m o ving away from this place. She could write anywhere, she had no family here, he had no one anywhere. They would end up starting their new lives together in a new place. The ol' throw the dart at the map and start over.

Jamie would want to talk to Pete first. Finding a partner in that line of work, a partner that you trust, is not easy. Pete was a couple of years older, but he had been at this for several years longer than Jamie. He had always been the one man on the ground when he collected. Several months after Jamie had started, he was sent with Pete to visit a number of gamblers that had made egregious errors in judgement on how much money they had to bet. Jamie was not happy, but Pete sold it as he could hang back and learn.

Pete had looked at him with this bemused look. Somewhere between *yeah right* and *you bet your ass you're going to learn something!* So, they rode together in Jamie's car. Pete spoke to him about the job, about how he enjoyed working for the King. In this area, the King's men all got r e s pect from everyone. Pete spoke of not always having to hurt someone; the job was being an effective collector and messenger. Jamie found that interesting. Collector was an idea he understood, but messenger... That one had gotten his attention.

"Okay, Pete, I get collector. But messenger?" Jamie was actually curious and would end up learning a few things that night.

"Okay, man. So, a lot of what we do is hurt people that steal money from the King. Everybody knows that part when they see us. But sometimes, we just have to speak firmly. Find out what the facts are. Now, if we have gotten our message across properly and no or very little money is involved… The King hates people that steal his money. Anyways, as I was saying, delivering a strong message keeps repeat offenders from clogging up our schedule."

Pete, if anything, was proud of the work he did. "So, tonight is a big message night. A group of eight guys that run a shitty strip club on the east end. They've been slinging out of there for the King for a couple years. Then, three months ago, they started coming up short. Not a ton just yet, but their count has come up short, nonetheless. The King wants a message sent before these dummies get themselves into too much debt. So tonight, two things are going to happen. One, we collect what they came up short. And two, one of them is going to get roughed up, but only just a bit. Remember, it's a big message night!"

"Understood." Jamie spoke with confidence. "But how do we know that they will all be there?"

"Good question, my man." Pete was beginning to like him, and Jamie knew it by the way he had spoken to him. "It's Saturday night, and every Saturday night they play cards in the back office of their club."

"Good." Jamie wanted to impress Pete. "Do you know the doormen there?"

With a smile, Pete nodded and stared ahead as Jamie turned up some eighties pop. They drove the last few miles in silence, both lightly bobbing their heads to the sounds of Hall and Oates.

The Velvet Spittoon was a classless dive of a strip club. Spittoon was a good name, as the dancers would spit or swallow for an extra twenty bucks. The joke amongst the bouncers was that the floors cracked at the end of the night from all the crusty cum.

It was dark, the entire private dance area smelled of rotten twat covered with Dollar Store perfume, and a cornucopia of cum. Only lonely men that couldn't ever get a date and didn't know where to find hookers found their way into the "Easy Spittoon," as it was called by those that frequented it.

This wasn't the place to find the young and handsome crowd. The dancers were mostly middle-aged mothers trying to make ends meet, and the owners were just pushing drugs through the doors. No one really counted all the money the customers paid the women. The drugs were the bigger part of the club owners' income; the lifeblood of the club were the junkies that came in and out buying The King's drugs. Sadly, a lot of the club's dancers were more about the drugs than they were about making ends meet at home. Thus, is life at the bottom of the ladder.

As Pete and Jamie pulled up for their first job together, they briefed one another on what each of their part of their jobs was. It was a habit that they continued on every job they worked together after that first night. Pete walked directly to his guy at the door. They stared at one another briefly and the man invited him to enter.

Pete leaned in to whisper something very quickly to the man. nodded as his eyebrows shot up. Jamie later found out that he told him the boys in the back had fucked up one too many times, but tonight was just a message, the only message.

Jamie and Pete were not your typical Spittoon customers. They were well dressed and fit. They appeared to have money and walked with confidence. The ladies flocked to the money immediately. In the strip club, money got more attention than a big dick any day! The men continued toward the back office; they were ready to do the job the night called for them to do, they were prepared for the worst to happen. *All professionals*, Jamie thought to himself, *were always prepared for things to go tits-up*. The King's men were always prepared for the worst. Pete would go on to tell Jamie of some fucked up situations he'd walked into alone, but he was always prepared. That's what he would preach to him over and over as their partnership continued. Always be prepared for anything that might go wrong. The eight men in that room were not connected in any way to anyone important, just a group of friends from college. There were a couple of bigger weightlifting white guys, three Mexican guys who didn't speak Spanish, and three black guys that had started the club. They needed capital, and their five buddies wanted to buy into the business. The name Velvet Spittoon was the idea of one Mexican guys. His grandfather loved watching old westerns in the living room with him, and the bars always had a spittoon and the dancing girls upstairs. So, "Velvet" was thrown in to give it a kinky spin and thus was born what would become the dirtiest strip club in the city. Like everything else in life, it started as a nice place, but nothing stays pristine when poor businessmen are trying to run it. They wanted good-looking women, women that didn't whore themselves out during private dances, and it was going to be a classy joint. Eight months in, six of the eight owners were snorting up over half of the funds coming into the club. They were buying from the King; none of these snot noses knew a thing about dealing drugs. What they knew was spending money and doing drugs!

The King was a mystery man to most people, including the DEA, local police, and the ATF. Many had gone after him, but he only spoke to his circle. No one that he didn't know had any way to approach him. Not new dealers, collectors, or suppliers. He had not spread his circle in many years. The King could be sitting next to the mayor at a city function, and no one would know. Powerful wasn't even the word for this man. Law enforcement called his network Godlike and untouchable.

So, these six men approached their dealer, telling him that they needed to "make money." As a smart dealer, he heard money.

"Let me see what I can do. How much longer can you stay open with what you guys got?"

Philip, one of the weightlifters, spoke up. "Maybe another two weeks or so. Come on, man, please help us."

"I'll see what I can do for you, Philly."

It ran up the chain quickly; an entire club selling their product was an extremely lucrative offering. Within hours, the smallest circle had gotten the word back down to the street hustler.

The word was, they would take only what they could sell—any fucking shortages would not be taken lightly. (That was one warning the shitbags had apparently not taken seriously.) They sold product only to those they knew; once it left their hands, it didn't matter, as they had plausible deniability regarding any drugs having ever been in their club. With that said, they could invite the people that would buy from them into the club. The dancers were not to be involved in any way with any deals. Ever. The owners were the only dealers in that place. Should anything come up with any dealings, it was best that no more than two of them be there on any given night. This was another rule that had been ignored.

So, three years later, the club was a complete shithole. The dancers willing to work there were nowhere near the type that had been there in the beginning, and the six cokehead owners were now eight cokehead owners.

For six nights out of the week, they did keep it to just two of the guys, but on Saturday nights it was all eight for their, not so secret, weekly card game. Something that they had done since college and saw no reason to stop, even though they were warned not to all be in the same space at any time. Sometimes you live and learn, tonight did not seem to have that floating in the air. Tonight, would be a "you fucked around, now you find out" type of night.

So tonight, their game would get interrupted by the two men, that anyone who had ever crossed the King didn't want to meet. Sure, there were whispers of the King's muscle, but only rumors. The King's collectors were ghosts until you crossed a line. The thing to remember was that no one met them more than twice. If you got to a second visit it was done.

As the two men came to the office door, they took a moment, looked at one another to assure that they were ready for anything that might happen after they entered that door. Pete told him that his rule of thumb was that things don't ever happen according to plan. Jamie smiled at his partner as they went to open the door.

Pete grabbed the doorknob and, yes, it was unlocked; imagine a bunch of druggies worrying about locking the door. As they opened the door, they were stared at by a gaggle of bleary eyes. They didn't say a word at first. They looked at Pete and Jamie as if they might be ghosts. Then came the same tough guy statements, bravado, and bullshit that they men had heard over and over:

Who the fuck are you guys?

What the fuck are you doing in here?

Do you know who we are?

Yeah, we work for the King!

It was the last statement that caught Pete's attention. "Excuse me, but you work for who, exactly?"

John, formerly a buff weightlifting guy, now a skinny scabby junkie, spoke up. "Yeah, fuckface, we work for the King. So, you get your ass out of here or we'll get him on the phone, and you two fuckers are dead."

It would have been funny if the man had not said the King's name. While Pete was deciding what to do next, Jamie decided to count the men. Something was wrong, there were only seven there. What they hadn't yet noticed was that one of the Mexican guys was not at the table. He was, in fact, in the private unmarked bathroom. He had heard John speak up. And he knew that unwelcome people in their area could not be good. He grabbed the group's gun from inside a box that was under an old stack of Hustler magazines. They kept it there just in case anything ever went wrong in the club. And somebody that arrived uninvited inside their office was not good. In his drug-addled brain, he thought he was Clint Eastwood. He would open the door and take out whoever was out there.

Stepping away from Pete, Jamie began to look around. There were two rooms. Neither had anything written on the door, so he chose the right. The door was locked. He shot a quick knowing glance at Pete; his look said enough as Pete began to count the men at the table.

Just then, Felipe had come from the private bathroom housed behind the door on the left and had drawn a gun on Pete.

Felipe never saw Jamie coming. He moved so fast, even Pete had been surprised that the man never got a shot off before a bullet hit the side of his head. His friends screamed; again, it was funny listening to seven drug fiends screaming because they heard a shot and that these same men had been so full of bravado just half a minute earlier. Pete, seeing the man hit the ground, sprang into action immediately. He shot the two men closest to him. Jamie put holes in the heads of four others. The lucky man left alive,

Mike Wilson, one of the first two that wanted to open the club, sat in shock. His best friends were all dead. He was high and scared, which made him feel sick to his stomach, and his buzz was immediately gone. Pete was now in charge of everything that would happen for the remainder of their time in the office.

"Where's all your money? Not part, and not even a cent short of every penny that you have in this office. Do you understand me?"

Mike was in tears, grabbing his temples like a hulking migraine had suddenly hit him, Pete did not like repeating himself; so, with a slap he asked once again, "Fucko, you have five seconds to answer. After that, I'll fucking look around and find it myself. Speak!"

"It's in that locked office," Mike cried in a

trembling voice. "The key is in Ramon's pocket."

Pete laughed and spoke up again, "Which one of the dead people is Ramon?"

"He's right there, sir." He pointed at one of the men that Pete had just killed.

"I got it," Jamie said and dug into the pockets of the recently deceased Ramon. Grabbing the key, he walked to the back office on the right and unlocked the door.

The idiots literally had a room full of money. They had stolen money, chosen to just leave it wide open, and, worst of all, were throwing the King's name around. It was a trifecta of fuckery.

Along with the money, there were still drugs left to return to the King. It would go neatly back to where it belonged. And, unfortunately for Mike, he would be donating his tongue to the King. This was the first time Jamie would see this, and it disgusted him far too much, but he would get used to it. Right? It was going to be the job.

Pete, by this time an old hand at this, knelt on Mike's chest hard enough to make him lose his breath and open his mouth wide to breathe. Pete deftly squeezed the crying man's jaws and, in an instant, had cut his tongue out. He let the man lay there bleeding and crying for what seemed like an eternity to Jamie.

Mike thought to himself after Pete stood up and put his tongue in a container that the two men were going to let him live. He sat up and continued to weep; he tried to stop the bleeding with his shirt.

"You know, man, it didn't have to be this way. Everybody tries to steal, we know that, but you clowns made the shit obvious," Pete said calmly, but with a bit of candor as he pushed a body onto the ground and took their seat. "You see, stupid people always want too much. You had your club, you were selling a little blow, and your doors stayed open. But you got greedy."

Pete stood up and walked over to Jamie, and they spoke quietly for just a moment. Jamie kept an eye on the tongueless man on the floor as they did. Pete put the box holding Mike's tongue into the pocket of his overcoat. Jamie put his hand on the doorknob but stopped short of opening it. The two men then turned and faced the still-crying man.

Pete looked at Mike for a moment and spoke softly, "And you never worked for the King, you really fucked yourself on that one, kid. This was just supposed to be a message... a message."

Jamie had levelled his weapon and fired three rounds, quickly, into the man—two to the head and one to the chest.

They locked the office from the inside and left the back, heading toward the front door, both double-fisting duffle bags. No one had been disturbed, as the music shook the entire building until about 2:30 in the morning. Pete stopped and spoke quickly to the door man, slipped him some cash, and the men walked away.

"What did you tell the guy at the door?" Jamie asked as they settled in the car after putting everything in the trunk.

"I told him paychecks wouldn't be written tonight, and he might go ahead and take the rest of the night off. And here were the funds he and his crew might be missing, in case anyone asks if he knew what happened," Pete said with a grin. "He'll be at a new club door in a couple of weeks."

"Nice." Jamie was ready to press on as he

cranked the car and looked to start his music.

"You know, Jamie? That was great work in there. I didn't get the count, and he got the drop on me. I got comfortable and shit didn't go as planned. Thank you."

"Anytime, man. We're partners, right? We got to look out for each other." That was that the men were partners after that night.

Word got to the two men that the King was very happy with the recovery of the money and the bonus drugs. Being good collectors meant doing the right thing every time they went out.

Visit after visit, the men were becoming very adept at doing the job right on the first go. They were the most used and effective collectors. It paid well and kept them busy. The people that entered into agreements with the King knew the line not to cross. If they did cross the line, there were consequences from the men that protected the line.

They were the line's protectors. It was difficult to explain, but put simply, they went to any extent to pull back those that had crossed that virtual line of whatever crime they were doing and giving the right amounts back to the right people.

You get into the drug game; sure, what you're doing is a crime, but there are levels to the criminals involved. If you knew the junkies or sold on street corners—dime bags, rocks, the little stuff, you were near the bottom of the ladder. Then came the guys that supplied you, and the further up the ladder you went, the circle grew smaller and exponentially richer. These people were invisible to the general public, very rich and untouchable.

They drew the lines, they made the rules, and

guys like Jamie and Pete, well, they pulled those ignorant enough to cross those lines back into the playground. Too often, Jamie thought, it ended with a tongue in a box that was passed through the hands of about ten people till it arrived at the top of that ladder.

Jamie was always surprised by the levels of violence that he was able to achieve with these people. He had never really been violent. Sure, he'd had his share of fights growing up, didn't we all? But, again, killing a person for the first time? Going into his first few collections, he was told it might happen. Just be cool, do what must be done and it will all fall into place.

The guy in the Spittoon was not his first customer that he had killed. That happened on his first night out as a solo collector. The guy was just supposed to be a message recipient that night. It all went sideways because he wanted to look tough for his buddies.

"We'll fucking stand out here and talk," he'd brashly said he collector.

"Look, I think that we should take it inside for a bit of privacy." Jamie, if nothing, was typically a gentleman on each occasion, he thought of Patrick Swayze's words in "Roadhouse" be nice 'till it's time not to be nice.

"You afraid of my boys? Cause we'll get rowdy!" Again, bravado. Later in his career, Jamie would grow to enjoy the bravado. Some of the things these people said were pretty funny given the context of what was about to happen to them. And seeing a tough guy cry was sort of therapeutic. It's the change in dynamic. In a moment they went from knowing everything was fine, that they were in charge, to wondering if the man that just beat them in front of family, friends, and others was going to end their life.

Calmly, Jamie spoke again, "I think it's best that we step inside, your employer has a message for you."

The man spoke loudly but never got a complete word out. Jamie grabbed him by the scruff of his shirt collar. One of his jobs was to be discreet about who his employer was. Names were not used in a public environment. So, the shirt grab was merely to show the gentleman the imminent seriousness of his situation. Still, tonight was just to be a stern message once they got inside. Then Jamie heard a bottle break.

The brash man's friends, the man, and Jamie were the o n l y people present. So, a bottle breaking meant one of them had just gone off the reserve. Jamie made some quick business decisions. Dumb drug dealer was hit with a hammer fist to the nose; he dropped, crying out in pain, nose bleeding, and blinded by the immediate flow of tears caused by the hit. Next, would-be Mr. Broken Bottle. For that, Jamie spun, reaching his shoulder holster for his weapon.

When Jamie entered any room, on the job, took a mental picture of each person's position. He found it interesting that women seemed to think that they were above getting the business end of a weapon or fist. Work was work and Jamie was good at what he did. Typically, when faced with a stressful situation, people stand still. They subconsciously freeze, all of the big ideas of what they would do in dangerous times all leave them. Jamie's o n l y mover would be likely be holding the broken bottle. Even before he had spun around, he had an idea which he men it was that had just gambled his life away. Upon observing the room as he walked in, there was the tough guy of the bunch—tight cranberry chinos, loafers with no socks, a loud silk shirt, and hair that a tornado couldn't move (likely a combover thought Jamie). If that didn't shout "I'm a peacock," all his jewelry finished the statement.

So, the messenger became the collector as he spun to reveal his weapon in his left hand. Three men were still in place like mannequins, and there was Jamie's peacock with the broken bottle in his hand. Jamie grinned widely; the peacock's feathers began to fall quickly.

Some people, in the face of danger, step up and face down whatever they've gotten themselves into. These people are the true tough ones. It's that, "I'm in till the end, fuck it!" mentality. They're gritty and you'll get some fighting spirit from them.

Mr. Peacock, though, was on the other side of that coin. He started backing down, crocodile tears welled in his eyes, and as they rolled down his face thick enough to make his spray tan run a bit. He politely placed the bottle on the table that he had used to break it. Jamie made a quick decision: that man would have to die. Nothing personal, but these men did not hang out with the bleeding guy on the ground for his company. They knew what did, who he probably did it for, but they didn't know the consequences of insulting those men or their collectors. One thing he knew from day one was never to make your boss look weak. He put three bullets in the man's chest and told the other men that the first one to move got three of their own.

Walking back to his original customer, he said angrily, "Look at me, dumbass. This was just a reminder visit. You've been light on three collections. Don't let there a fourth. Next time I come, I won't spend any time talking to you. This will be your only free visit, next time it will cost you more than money. Now, send the money that you owe, and it better be there before I'm in my car."

As he turned to walk away, he thought for a moment. "Clean up this mess, get your buddies to take care of tough guy over there. Trust me, this night ends better with you doing that. You don't ever want to see me again."

The three men still frozen in time were spurred into action by the homeowner. "Go on, guys, let's get this cleaned up. I'm sending the money right now," he yelled after the man that was making his way through the side gate.

Jamie took a quick breath. That was a lot more work than a message. First night, first kill. It was not what he had expected, but he had done it without hesitating. He was glad of that. Ronnie, the outer circle guy that had brought him in when word got around that he was looking to be a messenger or collector, told him the first kill would be the toughest. But there was no worry, the first few visits were only messages. It was to gauge if he was able to project the type of intimidation that needed to be put out there by their men.

"What the fuck just happened in there? Jesus H. Christ!" he exclaimed. That got out of control too quickly. He called Ronnie right away for two things: Was the money there? And to inform him that someone had been killed. Ronnie laughed and told him the money was, indeed, there. Secondly, Ronnie let out another quick laugh. "First night? That guy was supposed to be a big pussy. What happened?"

Jamie explained the entire situation, that it hadn't been the greedy prick that ended up dead, but a tough guy with more muscle on his arms than between his ears.

"It's fine, Jamie," Ronnie reassured him. "It happened. I'll be reaching out via another messenger about that happening to you."

"Thanks, Ronnie. I appreciate you trusting me with this job."

"You're good, my man, have a nice night. I'll be in touch when we have more work for you. Goodnight!"

"Goodnight," Jamie said and hung up the phone. He got his car going and headed home. He didn't drink very often; in a year he could count the number of times he drank with one hand. He liked feeling in control. Still, tonight would require a couple of drinks. After that night, he was ready no matter how crossed up things got.

All these years later, and meeting Sandy was really the first time that he had thought the job had run its course. He sat staring into her eyes as she spoke about all the things she had planned for the future. The writing awards that had yet to be won. Travelling the world and starting a family. On mentioning a family, she had stared at Jamie to gauge his reaction. He smiled at her and gave her a slight nod, the seal of approval that he also wanted a family, in the future.

"Do you ever think of leaving here?" Jamie thought he may as well start dropping hints.

Sandy thought for a moment. "Yes, I can write anywhere. And travelling would make me more knowledgeable about the world. Now, why do you ask, Mr. Man?"

Caught, Jamie decided to be honest. "It's only been six months—"

"Six and a half, sir," she said as she laughed.

"Okay, six and a half months." He grinned. "But, Sandy, my job might be ending in a while. I want to get into another line of work. And, just like you, I can find work anywhere. What would you think of finding a new place in the world together?"

"Well, aren't you full of surprises tonight?"

"Oh, just wait, I'm a surprise and a half!"

They both laughed, enjoyed their dinner, and spoke of a life together for the remainder of their evening. As they began to fall asleep, he thought that his next conversation would be with Pete, his best friend, since the fateful night of their first meeting.

The two men, although good friends, rarely saw one another outside of work. They had the occasional breakfast or lunch. Sometimes a drink and a cigar at an old cigar pub downtown.

"You called for this meal at this ungodly hour,

so it's on you, buddy!" Pete laughed as they stared at their breakfast menus.

"Of course, I know the rules, my man. Do your worst!"

They smiled and began to prepare their coffee to drink. But Jamie knew that Pete didn't like much to change the schedule, and calling this breakfast was a curveball.

"All right, kid, what's going on? You hate being up early as much as me."

"Pete, I'm thinking of moving on from collecting. I've met someone, and I think that it might be the time for me to relocate and start over."

Pete frowned for a brief moment, then he smiled. "Nice, kid, that's something I never got around to when I was still in the market for someone to spend my life with. I'm happy for you. Does she know what you do?"

"No. Hell no! I always keep our world to myself. No, I sold myself as a collector. I'm careful."

"Good. Have you talked to Ronnie yet?"

"No, you're my partner, and I needed to talk to you first. You're an important person to me. I need to be sure we're good before anything else. So, are we good?"

"Jamie, I'm happy for you, and yes, we're good. Always good." Pete raised his cup of coffee and air-toasted his friend.

The remainder of breakfast was banter—never shop talk, just small talk. They parted ways with a one-armed half-hug. As Jamie began to walk, Pete sat down to finish his last cup of coffee. He waved at his friend and watched him walk through the door in a great mood.

Pete let out a short breath, took a drink of

coffee, then placed the cup on the table and took out his phone.

Jamie, fresh off talking to Pete, was feeling ready to speak with Ronnie later that night. He would spend the afternoon speaking with Sandy. Beginning to make plans, where did they want to live. Surprising to Jamie, Sandy was just as ready to begin life together.

It was such a relief; they both seemed to be on the same page. Sandy might need a month to finish up a few articles locally, resign, and close out her lease at her apartment. The thing about Jamie was he was like a lot of people on the surface. He paid his bills on time, shopped for groceries, was a quiet and neat neighbor, and floated along like he was just another guy. But who Jamie really was is a man that always looked over his shoulder, lived in an unassuming apartment well away from everything that looked rich or was anywhere near anyone he would ever collect from. Living in a suburb was perfect for hiding his work life from his real life. In the end, though, he was always ready to drop everything and be gone in an hour.

He felt that leaving this life would be easy. He had saved most of his money over the years. He had it spread all over the world, and one small duffle bag with enough to start until he needed to access any one of his many accounts. As the evening fell upon him, he dressed for his meeting with Ronnie. He looked at himself in the mirror, double-checked that he had everything he needed. He patted himself down and felt ready to go.

On the ride into the city, he went over what he wanted to say to Ronnie. Over and over, word by word he wanted to be succinct. He found that he was a bit more nervous than he thought he might be. He pulled up to this beautiful building and went around the corner to park on the street. He would use the walk to relax a bit. It also helped him to look about the cars on the street, a habit he'd gotten over the last few years of his work. Never walk into any space without looking at everything that the surroundings have to tell you.

Ronnie did all of his business from a penthouse apartment in the center of downtown. It oozed class. Still, Ronnie hadn't the least bit of ostentatiousness about him. His things were nice, but not too nice. No loud paintings or furniture. He was very confident and always kept a guard inside his door.

Jamie rang the bell, and a large man opened the

door.

"Vincent, how are you doing? Goddamn, my man, are you lifting the entire gym?" They briefly shook hands and smiled at one another after sharing a quick laugh.

"Doin' good, Jamie. Good to see you. Ronnie is in his office."

"Thanks. See you in a bit." Jamie immediately began moving toward the apartment's office.

As respectful as ever, he quietly knocked on the door and waited for Ronnie to ask him to enter.

"Come in, Jamie." Ronnie had a wide smile on his face. "On time as usual. Boy, but aren't you punctual? Have a seat. Would you like a drink?"

"No, sir, I've got a date tonight. Thank you." Jamie's voice was confident, but he felt a lump in his throat.

"Okay, my friend, so what's on your mind?" Ronnie reached into his humidor and pulled out a beautiful-smelling Cuban cigar. As Jamie began to speak, Ronnie got his cigar clipped and lit.

"Well, Ronnie, I've met someone. I'm interested in moving on from collecting. We want to start a new life, but to do that, I can't continue to do this."

"Wow, congratulations, Jamie." Ronnie was taking a drag on his cigar and blowing the smoke up into the air.

"Thank you so much, Ronnie. I appreciate everything that you have done for me. I spoke to Pete this morning. He knows, and I just wanted to let you know before I moved forward. Thank you for taking this meeting. I'm going to head out unless you need anything else from me?"

"You know, Jamie," Ronnie stood and walked to his large window, "your friend Sandy is a very beautiful lady."

Since the first time that he had taken a life, Jamie was rarely surprised. Ronnie saying Sandy had almost knocked him off his feet. Jamie felt that he hid his surprise quite well, but how long could he bluff?

"The thing is, the King really doesn't like to lose employees." Ronnie turned to him and gave him a long stare.

"Look, Ronnie, we never talked about me leaving, but you left out the part about the job being a permanent position. Is there an amount of money that can end this?"

Jamie knew that money often spoke to the

more powerful men in the dope game. Still, offering money right away was a risky play, but it was his only play at that moment.

With a laugh, Ronnie sat heavily in his chair and let out a long sigh. "Sorry, there's no buying your way out of this. The problem is, the King feels that you know of too many of the skeletons in his closet. You and Pete have done a lot of hard work over the years; plus you are one of the best collectors he has."

"But, Ronnie, you know me. I'm a private person. Sandy knows nothing about what I do. I just want to start a new life."

"I'm sorry, kid, but she's a fucking reporter. A reporter? What did you think would happen? But, if it makes it any better, there's no future there anyway."

Jamie didn't like the tone, and it incited a quick

response. "What does that mean?"

"Stay calm, but once we found out about your activities, we took action."

Not being unreadable at this moment could work for or against him, but Jamie spoke up with his first hint of anger. "What is that supposed to mean? And don't bullshit me, Ronnie!"

"A couple of collectors picked her up after the two of you parted company earlier."

The revelation sparked fury under Jamie, a fury that he had never felt before. As Ronnie spoke, Jamie's mouth began to open.

"Now, just relax. No one can risk her knowing anything, you have to understand. People rarely leave this life, and if they did, how does it look if you're playing house with a reporter?"

Two things quickly crossed Jamie's mind, and

not much time was left for him to be here. First thing, how did he know her name and what she did? Second, where were they taking her?

"Look, Ronnie, none of that is necessary. She writes articles on fashion and lifestyle. She doesn't have any type of contacts into crime. They're fluff pieces. Christ, Ronnie, isn't there anything we can do?"

"Look, she'll be visiting with the King soon, don't worry. It'll be over very quickly."

"What the fuck did you just say?" Jamie shot up and could no longer hide his anger.

"Look, Jamie, you wanted this life. You wanted the money. Now, walking away is rare. But just thinking that you can walk away, not happening."

"You just fucked up."

"Now, buddy, you might not want to do that."

A familiar voice from behind him. Pete. What just happened?

Time for quick thinking. Pete had been with Ronnie for even a bit longer than him. He was quite faithful to Ronnie, but speaking with him this morning, was that a mistake?

Yes. Yes, it was a big fucking mistake. Pete asked a lot of questions, and Jamie had eaten it up. Did he really think that he genuinely wanted to know about his future life? Fuck!

"Pete, you set this up?" Jamie spoke slowly and kept his hands at his sides as he turned sideways, giving himself the ability to see both men easily.

"Ronnie and I have been friends for many years. And we fall into a circle several slots up the totem pole to the King. So, yeah. I am protecting our, uh…investments." Pete was smooth as ever, calm, and already had a weapon drawn.

While Pete spoke, Jamie was making business decisions in his head.

Vincent wouldn't head this way, as Pete was expected to fire his weapon. That would help.

Even with his weapon drawn, Jamie knew something that Pete had never known. Jamie was much quicker on the draw than he had ever shown. Even with his weapon out, unfortunately, Pete had no chance to get a shot off. They had spent time together over the years and Jamie had never shown himself to be as quick as he really was.

There was never a reason to. It was something he had just learned over the years: show the world just enough. If you try too hard, people expect too much. Besides, Pete felt important when he showed off his gun skills.

Ronnie needed to be alive, but not able to contact Vincent when Pete went down. Pete had already let him know that Ronnie knew where to find Sandy. Now it was go-time.

"Pete, why, man?" Jamie was not a big talker typically, so this might give him even more time.

"Kid, no one leaves clean. You should have known that." Pete spoke with no sense of remorse.

"I guess I should have known. You're right." Jamie sounded deflated.

"You were the best partner I ever had. I'm sorry." Pete managed to sound sad for a moment. Jamie's eye caught him beginning to raise his weapon.

"So am I."

When Jamie left home, as he stared at himself in the mirror and patted himself down, he had grabbed his weapon on the way out. He had never taken a weapon to Ronnie's place, but leaving an organization can sometimes be difficult. Vincent was an observant guard. If Jamie walked in with a weapon, Vincent would see it and likely collect it. So, being safe means being careful.

He always shakes hands, thought Jamie, so what would help was something he could keep on his arm. He'd never used it before, seen silly movies with an item like it being used. It was simple enough. Two Velcro straps around his arm held two bars that had a springlock with his weapon on the end. A sharp movement of his arm shot the weapon down into his hand. He'd tried it over and over, and it seemed to work every time. The true test was now, and it would have to work in the next few moments.

"Don't worry, I'll make it quick.?"

That would be Pete's last sentence. In fact, his last

words.

"Sorry, Pete."

Pete was confused for just long enough for Jamie to sharply move his arm downward. It appeared that he was trying to straighten his sleeves. Before Pete could utter a word, two bullets had entered his forehead. Jamie quickly

turned to Ronnie, putting a bullet in his knee, clearing his desk in a bound, and covering his mouth.

"Okay, Ronnie, I didn't think that it was happening like this, but you tell me how to get to Sandy in the next ten seconds, or you're going to suffer an utterly painful last few minutes of your life."

Ronnie had learned one thing about Jamie: he was not one to bluff when he said that he was going to make you hurt.

"Five seconds gone. You really want to suffer for

the King?"

Ronnie made his decision very quickly. "Look, Sandy will be on the 26th floor of the Brewer Building. The penthouse floor there is where the King will be. He's waiting for me to call to verify that you're gone. Then she's gone."

Jamie knew that if he was alive, the only thing stopping him from exacting God's revenge upon them was Sandy still being alive.

"You're a good man, Ronnie," Jamie said quietly.

"Tha—" Ronnie began.

Before he could finish, Jamie did what was right. He put a bullet through the bottom of his chin. Lights out.

Jamie stood. Four shots; Vincent would know that something had gone wrong. He'd have to be careful, but quick. If he knew one thing, the King would give a half an hour before he decided that the woman in his penthouse had outlived her usefulness.

He stopped and stared down at his "best friend." Pete was doing what he knew, nothing more and nothing less. In Pete's life, he had never trusted anyone, he was an aging violent man that did what he did out of greed and violent tendencies. Still, Jamie thought that he had become friends with the man, that they had shared good times, that they had truly connected. All of this hurt Jamie but killing Pete was the worst part of it. They were partners. For all those years, they stood back-to-back and protected one another. Jamie knew that he could not wound him though. Pete alive was more than dangerous enough. The moment of the shot, he saw Pete's surprise. He did not know of the arm strap release or how quickly his partner could move. He had seen so many dead bodies in the last few years, he'd been shot, stabbed, and pepper sprayed. Still, seeing his friend lying there with two bullet holes in his forehead was the worst pain he'd felt in years.

No time to cry. He moved quickly from the office and encountered the giant man waiting for him. Neither man spoke nor moved for their weapon. Jamie spoke first. "No checks are going to be signed tonight."

Vincent looked to his left and motioned with his hand to show his weapon was on the table and then spoke quietly. "Understood. And you need to hurry. You know where you're going?"

"Yeah," Jamie replied, visually relieved. "And thank you."

The men nodded to one another. As Jamie passed him, he picked up Vincent's weapon and hurried downstairs.

Getting to the penthouse would be the easy part. Once there, it would be a mystery, but a straightforward layout. All the buildings around here looked the same once you stepped into the apartments on the upper floors.

Not knowing how many guards would be up front, how many in the King's office, or how Sandy was being held, the things he could not plan for, the details that he wished to have available when he went to a location. As much as he didn't like winging things, he was all that Sandy had right now.

A thought crossed his mind as he drove. *She'll leave me now.* A love wasted because all they knew was that she was a reporter. Not what she reported, where she

worked, or any other detail. He knew that business was business; so, it was time to ramp up for his arrival.

Anyone that had never killed might not know what it took to "get there," to be in the mental state to go in knowing that someone was dying at the end of the night. It wasn't music, drugs, alcohol, or any other external force. Jamie found that it was all in his mental preparation. He turned up the heat, rolled up the windows, and gripped the steering wheel like he wanted to choke the life out of it.

Driving fast enough to get there, but slow enough not to draw attention. A collector had one thing that he needed when he went to work: discretion. Move in the shadows, go unnoticed, and work with as few movements and distractions as possible. Jamie had mastered this. Carrying weapons in hidden compartments is a good way to find trouble if you stood out.

The air in the car was still. It was unbearably hot; his irritation and anger were flaring. The quiet of the ride, with only the sound of the road beneath him, was monotonously alarming. It put him on edge to feel this. His senses were alive now, his pores open from the heat, and as a bit of sweat came out, he felt hyper-aware of everything around him.

He was two blocks away from the Brewer building. The only thing that he could hope for was that he was still going to be a surprise guest. Jamie parked the vehicle, taking a moment to be centered, to fill his head with what needed to happen once he arrived. Seeing it happen in his head, where the guards might be. He collected weapons from a compartment in his trunk. As he walked toward the building, he continued to mentally move and find guards in different locations. As a way of keeping himself sharp upon entering buildings, he observed the best places for security personnel and exits. As he continued his thoughts on the next ten minutes, he thought to himself; when would he have to fire a shot?

The longer that it took to fire a weapon the more

time that he had in silence. If it went to shit right away, he would have to start running. Hoping to get to Sandy before anything happened to her. He had to think of every possibility.

Jamie had never thought of himself as particularly bright, but he had a passion for detail. Everything that he did, he carefully planned out. Surprises were for people that were ill-prepared to do the things that needed to be done. Sure, he'd jumped from job to job during his life, and it seemed that he was aimless. Truthfully, though, he had worked out hard and researched being a collector for a bit. Getting to Ronnie was a lucky stroke. Having Pete partner with him for those years was heaven sent. He had saved incessantly, and the money had been better than he had imagined. His plan was to leave in maybe two or three more years. Meeting and falling for Sandy had changed all of that.

He approached the building. Looking around the lobby, he only saw two concierge clerks. These men were not armed nor personal security. That served as a good thing for Jamie. That would speed up his ascension to the penthouse.

"Hello, sir, how can I help you?" The first man at the desk stood to greet him with a smile.

"Hello, I need to go to the penthouse." And now it was time to gamble. "Please tell them that it's Ronnie Bassett."

The only thing that he could hope for now that he chose this route was that these men didn't know Ronnie's name or hadn't seen him before. Jamie saw this as the biggest gamble of the night.

The second concierge, an older gentleman with salt and pepper hair and a slight accent, picked up the phone receiver on the desk. He spoke quietly for a brief moment, then hung up the phone and gave a small nod to man number one, before simply returning to his crossword puzzles. And then the man standing before Jamie spoke.

"Come this way, Mr. Bassett. I'll send you on up."

They walked toward the elevator. The man pressed the up button. When the elevator arrived, Jamie stepped in, and the man swiped his card, typing some numbers into a security keypad after.

"You'll be sent straight to the penthouse, Mr. Bassett. May I help you with anything before I send you up?" The young man spoke politely and all about customer service with a smile.

"No, sir. Can't wait to see my friends." Jamie spoke coolly and gave the man a brief nod and a half-smile as the doors slid closed.

Details and possibilities flew through Jamie's head as the elevator slid quickly up the building's floors. It was going to go quite quickly. He had to be prepared to move upon the door opening.

The dings of the floors passing began to slow. His left arm was ready to snap and send his weapon down; that would get the party started. Probably two guys at best, but he continued to think to himself, *Be prepared for the worst.* And then the final ding sounded as he thought of one more word.

Sandy…

The doors slid open, and it was a no-win situation before they finished. At least eight guns were pointed at him; he slowly raised his arms leaving him looking unarmed for the moment. It was something that he had thought of, hoped against hope that it would not fall this way. The old unwinnable situation.

Anyone who has ever gambled knows this situation. You hope that at least one thing goes well, one thing in the millions of little twists and turns that make your hand. The thing is, as long as the game is still being played there's a chance.

But why were they so prepared, and where was Sandy?

"The King would like to meet you, Jamie," a heavy-set older guard said.

All of these men looked like Vincent. Same dark suits, tall, muscly, and intimidating.

What Jamie couldn't do was act surprised in any way. You always have to look like whatever happened was something that had crossed your mind.

Another guard spoke as they began walking toward the rear of the expansive apartment. "Just keep your hands at your sides and we'll be good, do you understand?"

Jamie spoke; he was attempting to sound calm while looking around the room for any advantage he could identify. "Understood."

The two men that had walked ahead opened the large black double doors at the end of the hall. In that moment, Jamie's thoughts lost focus, and he realized that Vincent had called and told them that he was on the way. *Son of a bitch*, he thought. *I should have killed him.*

"Welcome, Jamie." A small man behind a large desk stood as he spoke.

Jamie's thought was of a singular focus, here is the King. It figures, a little man with lots of money equals someone that would call himself a king.

"Thank you, sir. Where is Sandy? Is she safe?" Jamie got right to the point.

"She's next door." He tilted his balding head to the left at a closed door. "She's fine for now, but not for long."

"She didn't do anything. She knows nothing of what I do, who anyone in my life is or anything about this organization." Jamie spoke like a telemarketer, not stopping moving along the script and looking for an angle. "Sir, if I know anything about how things work here, she was grabbed from behind, gagged and blindfolded. She's seen no one, knows only me, and I'm nobody."

Jamie still had nothing that was coming to him to use. So, he had to continue to speak, but he was running out of things to say. "I know that you're going to do whatever you want to me. But—"

"Let me stop you there." The King finally spoke. The small man spoke like what Jamie thought he would speak. Pompous, self-righteous, and beyond his abilities to intimidate.

"You fucking brought a reporter around my business. You fucked me and everyone around you. There is no way out of this for either of you. Do you understand me?"

Jamie was livid and couldn't hide it. Civility had passed. "What the hell? Why the fuck does it have to be like this? I did not betray you or anyone else."

"The King doesn't give a shit. You get that?"

The anger at this putz speaking of himself in the third person had actually brought his thinking back online.

"The King doesn't care, but I do, sir. What about money?" Money usually talked to people like this.

"Money isn't the matter, it's the principle.

Besides, after we're done, I'll be taking your money from you. You'll have no use for it." The man turned his back to everyone and spoke in a grandiose voice. "Jamie, do you know the difference between a king and a conqueror?"

This grandstanding asshole. Well, now Jamie had an angle. Let the asshole talk about himself, he seemed to love doing that.

"No, sir. What is the difference?" Jamie spoke, still looking for something that could help him. There were eight men around him, and this tough guy talking about kings and conquerors. Before the man spoke again, Jamie looked at the demure man's manicured hands. Never had a hard day's work in his life, and this tongue-collecting freak had probably never held a gun. He liked to make people do things for him. Jamie was starting to hate this guy even more in those moments.

More than likely, this pussy was a rich kid, found out that money talks for most people and drugs make the world go round. Having a bunch of muscle around you that calls you sir, cuts people's tongues, and does all sorts of vile things for you can make you feel powerful.

"You see, the king is forever. A conqueror will come along and try to take the land by force, and maybe for a bit they will do well. They may take a land or even two, but in the end, the king and his kingdom is forever."

As the last statement came out of his mouth, the man slowly turned around and smiled a very slimy smile at the desperate man standing across from him.

"Really, is that the difference, sir?"

Then in an over auspicious voice, the King spoke

while moving his arms about like an orchestra conductor, "Men, please send our friend here to meet his maker or tormentor, whichever it is. Put him out of my misery."

With that, he laughed a tiny man's laugh, turned his back, and waited for the work to be done.

Jamie couldn't do anything but think to at least take out the little man before he died. He was about to make his move, but before he could do anything he heard strange sounds.

The sounds were weapons hitting the floor. Jamie's eyes widened for a moment as he looked around at each man standing across from him. The eight men in their suits were dropping their weapons, and the oldest man spoke up.

"Vincent called us, told us to get you in the room." He was waving the other men out, "Should I assume no paychecks are getting signed tonight?" The man smiled and nodded as the men began to walk out of the office. Jamie turned around in time to see the color drain from the King's face.

The King now looked all of a tiny man in terror as he turned to see that his security had left. He looked like he wanted to reach for a weapon but then remembered he didn't know how to use a weapon.

"Okay, Jamie, money, right? You know that I'm loaded. I can overfill your pockets. Just the thing a newlywed would need. You and the lady walk out, you never have to look over your shoulders. You'll both be free."

"Do you know the difference between a king and a conqueror?"

"What?" the King spoke unsurely.

"It's the question that you just asked me. Do you know the correct answer?"

Jamie was slowly walking toward the man that had worked his way to the large chair behind his desk and was panicking. He had no other security. He had always had some sort of security there for him. As a kid, it was the big kids that wanted money that protected him. Money had made him feel powerful, and because of that he had never needed anything more.

"You see, a king, he walks onto a land and says, 'It's mine.' It doesn't matter if others live there, he just says it's his. He's the first to do this, and everyone just goes along. He's done nothing to really own that land or be the real ruler. This king sends warriors to take the land in his name. He claims to be a blueblood. Again, they say things like they're God's chosen, they have a right to rule, they think of themselves as all powerful. Strangely, they stay clean through all of this. It's the warriors that die. He says that his rule is the rule of the land and that it comes to him directly from God. Right?"

"Sure…sure, Jamie. Thank you for clarifying."

"I'm not done. Are you comfortable?"

"Yes. I'm comfortable. Thank you."

"Sure, I'm here to educate and make sure that you're comfortable. Now, as I was saying, the king claims that God has given him the divine right to rule."

Jamie continued, he had the time now, he was going to make this man understand how you don't put yourself on a throne and expect consequences.

"Now, a conqueror will lead their men into battle. They go where others have been and establish their societies and kingdoms. The difference then is that a conqueror doesn't just walk in and say a completely open land is mine. No, what they do is walk into an established society, kick everyone's ass, walk up to the king and tell him to stand up from his throne, and then they take off his head."

"Please don't kill me. I have a family. I can't defend myself from you. You turned my loyal men against me, what am I supposed to do?"

Jamie laughed and spoke again, "That's the thing there, Ki— You know what shithead, what is actually your name?"

"Delvin Ross. My name is Delvin Ross. My family lives outside of town. I have two kids."

"Okay, Delvin, your men were never loyal. You can't buy loyalty. You can never buy loyalty. You buy muscle, you buy skill, and you buy people to make you feel better about yourself. Loyalty is what Pete did for you and Ronnie, Delvin. He and Ronnie died trying to protect your kingdom. They were loyal to you. Now, what Vincent did when he called the head of your security about me, that's loyalty amongst men. The men in your security detail; yeah, they were never loyal to you."

"Okay, please. Please…"

"Delvin, would you have had mercy on me?" Here Jamie paused for a moment, "Be honest." Jamie would only play this game for a moment longer.

"No. They were all supposed to kill you, then kill the girl."

"Rare honesty, Delvin. I like it. You can learn how to be a better person." Jamie smiled at the man that was almost in tears behind the desk.

The King thought that this was the turn of the page that he needed. Jamie was going to let him walk. He would leave this life; it all seemed to be crumbling. Maybe he would start using his degree. Change and better his life.

"Thank you, I understand. I will be better, thank you for this second chance."

Jamie walked away from Delvin. He snapped his left arm and out came his weapon. He stared at the small, cruel man behind the desk and spoke softly, "Second chance?"

Delvin had a moment to see that he was nothing more than a little man with a lot of money. He had hidden behind doors, men, and drugs. Thirty miles from here, there was an indistinct house at the end of a tidy cul-de-sac where two young boys were in their room playing video games. A small, blonde, middle-aged but still quite beautiful woman was reading an old Stephen King book in her bedroom. She was waiting for her husband, Delvin Ross, an art dealer in the city that had a show tonight. The family never went, as he dealt with more adult-themed art pieces.

Delvin Ross had been an average student, bullied early on because of his size. He used money to buy protection, friends, and girls. He graduated from high school, then went to college and reinvented himself.

It started with weed; he got a couple of guys under him. Those guys, Ronnie Bassett and Pete Rogers, were more into the muscle side of dealing. Delvin loved these guys; they would move up with him. The money, types of drugs, and power began to change. Two years later, the three men had turned the small enterprise into a powerful movement.

Delvin would not step on anyone's toes; he moved to an untouched area. He avoided butting heads, at least on his way to becoming the King. Ronnie stopped the street stuff a couple more years inti their venture. But Pete felt like staying on the streets. He was a fine dealer. Then a few years later, it changed. He wanted to do a Ronnie-type job. That was all good for a few more years. A couple of years before Jamie had come onto the team, Pete was asked to become a collector to look after the people in the outer circles. It was like being back in college all these years later. He had created a very solid group of collectors. The day that the met Jamie, he liked the guy. He was eager to learn and loyal. And he truly had come to love Jamie over their years together.

Finding out that the young man was dating a reporter had disappointed him greatly. He didn't want to call Ronnie. But loyalty with his friends ran very deep. They had been together since the beginning.

After Jamie left, Pete looked at him leaving. He picked up his coffee, then made a phone call to Ronnie. Ronnie said that he was disappointed, that Jamie was a good man. Then he told Pete to hold fast while he ran this up the pole.

Six minutes later, after all of those years of work it only took six minutes, his cellphone rang. Jamie's fate had been decided. The King's men would pick up the reporter. It would be Pete's job to end Jamie after he arrived at Ronnie's place.

Pete accepted the job. He knew that he could take care of quickly and painlessly. Jamie would be careful, but Pete knew that he was faster than his friend on the draw and his gun would be out, it would be quick. The one thing that he had pushed back on was killing Sandy. Pete explained that he knew Jamie hadn't said a word about his job to her, and he didn't know enough about anyone above him to have shared anything of importance. It was the first, and apparently last, time that Pete had ever asked for anything contrary to what was asked of him. Six minutes later, a call came back. The King had denied his request. It fucking sucked, but it was what it was. Loyalty ran both ways with these three men. So, he would do his duty for his friend and the organization.

As he died earlier in the evening, he was utterly surprised by the fact that Jamie had been that quick. His last thought was, *"Way to go, kid."*

Years into all the business, the King was this shadow figure. It gave him the ability to do what he wanted with his family. Pretending to be an art dealer that sometimes-had night shows. When the organization needed a face to be the King, Delvin would be surrounded by muscle. He was smart, spoke fast, and kept his hands clean from any of the dirty stuff. It was a rare occasion when he was needed, but it served a purpose.

After word came from Ronnie that Jamie was gone, the girl would die.

While the King was awaiting Ronnie's call, his head of security received a call and stepped away, excusing himself.

When the concierge called and said that Ronnie Bassett was downstairs, the King knew one thing right away. His friend Ronnie hadn't used his last name when calling up to the penthouse ever. He prepared his men, told them that Jamie was a dangerous man. When all of them headed to the foyer to await Jamie, the King took a moment to be Delvin.

His two oldest friends had apparently died. All the years and shit that they had been through. In his long-privileged life, The King; Hell, Delvin had only ever counted on Ronnie and Pete. All of the shit in getting the business going, making the mystery man behind it all. Letting Delvin be the money while they walked the walk. He would fuck with this man and watch him die for the lives that he had lost tonight. He decided all eight men would shoot this prick. This would be the man's penance and the King's vengeance for his friends.

The things that run through your mind in the last moments of your life. His children would live in a world without their father. He'd never make love to his wife again. He'd loved her since the moment they met just before everything went big time. He'd kept it very simple. He gave them a very nice life, but he had more money than King Midas. They would need money, but he'd never paid a dime in taxes. Stupid, that he was thinking of them needing money. And for all of money hidden all over the world—tens of millions, not one soul outside of this man would have knowledge or access to any of it. It was in crypto wallets, foreign accounts under umbrella companies, and invested. Never had he once had an actual job as an adult. And no one knew of his accounts. They would find out that he had been murdered in the city. But that was all, then it would come out that the man's family fortune was gone. He and his wife had modest accounts but not enough to maintain any real life. In short, his family was completely fucked.

One thing that he had learned in college but never really thought about, just a fun fact for neighborhood BBQ parties—light travels about a million times faster than sound.

Delvin had never thought of why exactly it was such a fun fact for him. He thought to himself that everyone has that conversation starter. And that had been his, always.

Late forties with only moments left of his life, he was scared. That was all. For all of the things that he had asked men to do over the years, he had never once gotten any blood on his hands. Delvin was the man behind the scenes, the money man, he was clean. Or as clean as the man that orders executions and tongues could be.

Finally, he learned for himself that you don't hear the bullet that kills you. And he knew exactly why? The stupidest fact in the world was his last thought. He saw the sparks from the muzzle and never heard the shot that ended his life.

Jamie walked toward where the man had fallen.

Then, for reasons beyond his immediate comprehension, he shot the man twice more in the face. He wasn't angry, it wasn't vengeful; he had simply had enough of the prick.

He threw the gun down and ran toward the room where Sandy was being held. He opened the door and Sandy was crying. She was probably told that the next time the door opened it would be the end of her life. He attempted to calm her quickly.

"Sandy, it's me." He removed her blindfold and gag. "I'm so sorry, babe. I never meant for any of this to happen. I'm so sorry."

She slapped at him and pushed him away initially, then realized that he had saved her life. She had been told that once he was dead, she was next. And he was here.

"How did you get here, Jamie?" She spoke through

her tears.

"Sandy, I love you. I'd take on the world for you. I'm so sorry." He paused to breathe, "Let's get out of here."

He continued to untie her, and they stood to leave. He held her hand and led her out through the main office to the foyer where the men had left minutes earlier. It was all over. All the circles spoken of and the cloak and dagger; they were all done by three men. Only three fucking men. And Jamie had taken care of the three of them. For good.

Sandy spoke up. "Are we going to be okay?"

"We'll be fine. I need to stop by my place and pick up a duffle bag. We can head out after, if you still want to be with me?"

"Yes, let's go." Then like an intrusive afterthought, "I'll call work from whenever we stop. I can write from anywhere," Sandy said in a relieved voice.

She had a choice at that moment, but she knew two things. One of the men had stepped in said, "Your boyfriend is on the way, it's going to be okay. Sit still."

Second, he had come for her.

They drove through the night, heading west. Breakfast had been at a greasy spoon where no one gave them a second look. Jamie squeezed her hand, and she stared at him with a wide grin. Then he spoke.

"Marry me, Sandy. I'll spend our lives together making you happy and being happy that you want to be with me. Please."

She took a breath and uttered one word. "Yes."

He didn't really hear it at first, but he read her smile.

Jamie wasn't often very happy doing what he had been doing for the last few years. Money was not enough to make you happy. Jamie had found out that his life needed more. And Sandy would fill that need for him.

As the future unfolded, he made true on his promise. He worked every day to make their lives an adventure, to make it a good life for the both of them. Money would never be an issue. In the years ahead, there were the typical ups and downs, children, and a beautiful life that Jamie never thought that he had earned. But it was one that they made…

Still, on that morning they were just starting their lives. The adventures, travels, and children were all an unseen future. Right now, it was deciding between pancakes and waffles. They took their time eating and Sandy looked up at Jamie as she felt him staring at her.

"What?" Sandy said with a laugh.

"I love you. I really do, babe?"

She giggled, "I love you too."

The beauty of their love is the realization that life begins when you choose to start. When you want it to begin.

The Duality
Paradox

Peter was a veteran. A combat veteran. There are all types of veterans, some went to combat, others trained and never had to go. All gave of themselves, training to kill. It was a foreign concept, that many could never understand you leave home, and you are thrown into a giant room to share with forty other men, and you learn to shoot, shit, shower, and eat as a unit.

Peter was from Texas. He remembered the day that he realized that all those guys around him were from all over the country. Not everybody was from Texas, and it was strange. People had different accents, words, and attitudes. Some came to get money for school, others to get away from bad home situations, and others because they had nowhere else to go. Peter wanted school money and focus.

As Basic Training advanced, Peter learned that

there was a lot of yelling! As strange as it seemed, it was a form of indoctrination. They yelled louder than anyone else, all platoons tried to out-pride one another.

Pride. That's the beast that sits on soldiers' shoulders. The concept was: train harder, be louder, and prepare to kill faster.

After nine months in combat, Peter came home. Well, Peter physically came home. That was a bit more than some of his friends got. Peter had seen his friends come home in pieces, in body bags, but most had never come home mentally. Peter thought that he had a handle on it. He felt that his mind was intact, but you cannot unsee and undo what is done in combat.

There are supposedly rules in combat. The thing Peter discovered was that there was only one rule that everyone followed: survive.

Coming home, for Peter, meant finishing out his military career over the next two years. He got ready to get out and find something new to do with his life. Peter took his GI Bill and enrolled in a local school; like many other soldiers, he stayed near where he had served stateside. He would go on to study and successfully earn a bachelor's degree in social work, followed with a certificate specializing in substance abuse counseling.

Peter found that these classes and the theories that he learned helped him deal with his own demons. No, drugs and alcohol were not his demons. Peter's demons were the images of combat that he had brought home; the images that played in his mind over and over. It was daily work, but he was handling it.

Before he eventually found his first job, Peter needed to be very sure that he had a good grip on the things that tortured him at night. The things that gave him nightmares. He was working with all the tools in his toolbox. After six months, he knew it was time to go to work. He'd had enough to keep him afloat while he got himself together.

While in school, he met Holly. She was an Education and Mathematics major; her goal was to teach math at the secondary level. It was a complete coincidence that the two of them had been at a local secondhand bookstore in town. She was looking for old math theory books, and Peter was looking for books on PTSD and related anxiety disorders.

"Hello, do you work here?" Holly had walked up behind him, lost.

Before standing and turning around, Peter

began to speak. "No. Sor—" Then he turned and saw this beautiful woman that stood before him.

"That's okay, thanks," Holly replied.

"Wait, maybe I can help you find what you need. I'm here all the time shopping," he quickly lied.

"Okay, would there be a copy of any books on new mathematics from the 1970s?" Holly knew exactly what she was looking for.

A lost Peter looked at her blankly and noticed movement to his right, near the front of the store. It was the clerk that had welcomed him minutes earlier. He was mouthing and waving. Peter gathered all the way to the back, right, and third shelf.

"Follow me this way," Peter said to Holly. As he began to move, he looked over his shoulder and mouthed *thanks!* The clerk just laughed.

As they arrived at the back of the store, Peter

waved at the shelves like a gameshow model waving at the big prize. They found several books that matched what she was looking for, and Peter asked if he could help her find anything else.

"No thank you. I appreciate your help." Holly began to focus on the books.

"Oh, okay. Well, if, you're sure? I mean, I can hang out if you need anything else," Peter said nervously.

"No…" Holly said with a little laugh.

For a moment, Peter thought of walking away, then summoned some courage. "Would you like to have a coffee, juice, or dinner?"

She picked up a second book, turned to look at him, and brushed a bit of her red hair from her face. "You aren't a weirdo, are you?"

"No weirder than anybody else. I'm okay

though." He managed to smile.

They had a nice dinner, laughed a lot, found that they were close to the same age, and loved the same type of television programs.

They dated for just over one year. Holly graduated and was teaching school. Peter had one year to go, but they had decided to get married. Starting a life with someone was a really big step for him. He'd known that starting their lives together was a healthy thing.

When Peter graduated, he had explained to Holly how he needed a few months before going out there to go to work. After all their conversations, she knew what he had been through. She understood that it would be a bit of time. They agreed.

At the five-month mark, Peter started looking

for jobs. A few job interviews later and no job. He was becoming discouraged. Then the prison system called. They were hiring an entry-level substance abuse counselor, and they were offering him the position.

He asked them for an evening to review the official offer, and they agreed to that. It allowed Peter and Holly to celebrate the job. He called by 8:30 the next morning and accepted the offer.

Aside from the initial paperwork, drug testing, and background checks, the process went very smoothly. It was a week, and he was on the job.

He had sessions twice per day, three days per week. There were guards around him, and it felt like a physically safe environment for him.

"Good morning, men. My name is Pete Armstrong; I'm your counselor for our sessions.

You are invited to come into our sessions as often and for as long as you like."

He paused and went over the basic rules. "This is a safe space to share your experiences, issues, or past problems with substances. Now, if you do admit any new crimes, I am responsible for reporting that. With that being stated, is anyone ready to begin sharing?"

It started slowly. Peter had a bit of conversation with different prisoners. Asking names, how long they had been sober, little questions for starters. Then the conversation started flowing.

The session went well, and the next few sessions went well. The prisoners seemed to like the new counselor. But, as is life, someone always wants to push. The one pushing on this day was a man named Simon Bonner. Bonner was in for life; he had killed his wife and children on a night when he was high.

As everyone settled in, Peter sat down. He asked the prisoners how they were, how sobriety was, and what their goals were for the week. Then Bonner started in on him.

"I hear you were in the Army, Doc. Is that true?"

"First of all, I'm not a doctor, and yes, I was in the Army for three years," Peter responded as he smiled. For the danger he had learned to sense, he didn't feel this one coming. He was ready to move onto something else.

"Wait, I'm not ready to move on yet. You ever kill anybody?" Bonner was pushing buttons that he didn't know that he shouldn't be pushing. Peter knew to move away from the topic of his service.

"Let's talk about our sobriety plans. David Smith, how are you doing?" Peter was attempting to move fast.

Bonner continued pushing, and Peter was running out of places to run away. "Come on, man, you know everything about us. I killed four people. I'm here for life. So how many on your resume?"

Peter paused, then he felt like he was pinned into a corner and then began to speak with purpose. "Okay, I'll play for just a moment. I don't know how many.
Somewhere north of ten but less than twenty. We good?"

"Whoa, we got a regular Dahmer here. Look at this guy. Come on, man, I killed four people, and I get life. What did you get, a parade?"

Bonner's eyes were burning holes in Peter. He thought that he had a foot up on the counselor. Bonner was the classic narcissist, feeling like he was always the one in charge of the situation. Bonner did not know the man he was pushing was not well.

"No, no parades. A few medals, some awards, and a giant coin. Is that what you really want to know? Or do you not really want to know anything? I know people like you, you push because you think that people will not push back. Am I right?" In his controlled demeanor, Peter was pushing back.

Bonner was surprised, a bit shaken, but couldn't look bad in front of everyone. "Look there, Mr. Armstrong, I'm just a run of the mill criminal. I'm no big-time killer like you. I was just asking questions."

Peter was hiding how he felt but knew if he let this man push him it would go on in every group session. Prisoner after prisoner, it would get worse, so he made a decision to defend himself.

"Sure, I'll fill you in on what you want to know." He had raised his voice just a bit and a guard made a move forward. Peter waved him down. "I killed soldiers who wanted to and tried to kill me. I killed people who attacked me, made a move at me or a move toward anyone in my platoon. We killed when it was necessary." He took a breath and continued, "Now, you…you killed a woman and two children, right? Were they trying you? Threatening you? No, I think they were asleep, right? People sleeping are scary, especially kids."

"Look, Armstrong, watch your mouth," Bonner warned, but he didn't know he was the one in real danger.

"I'm just making an observation, right? You killed unarmed people that were not trained to fight back. You sound a lot like a coward to me. Yeah, you know,

Mr. Bonner, you are a coward. Tell me, does it get you a lot of street cred in here to be a child killer?"

Bonner moved with deceptive quickness, but Peter was much faster. He had him on the ground and a hand on Bonner's throat before the guards had moved. The choke was tight enough so that Bonner was scared and was actually relieved when the guards placed their hands on Peter's shoulders. He immediately released and stood up. But he never lost eye contact with Bonner—he wanted the seed of fear that he had planted to take bloom.

Officer Brian Reynolds was the first to get to Peter. As Peter stood, Reynolds asked, almost laughing, "You okay, Mr. Armstrong?"

"Yes, I'm good, thank you officer. Please remove Mr. Bonner. He cannot return for two weeks. Oh, and Mr. Bonner, hopefully I'll see you in two weeks." Peter meant what he said to the man, but he felt good for having stood up for himself.

At the session's end, Peter was summoned to the warden's office. As he walked toward the office, he felt like he had fucked it all up. The warden, though, told him that he was glad that he had stood up for himself. The last counselor had left after being verbally pushed by convicts and not having a decent way of defending themselves, verbally or otherwise.

"You won't be having any more problems after today, Mr. Armstrong. Good job, enjoy the rest of your shift and have a nice evening. Remember, you did nothing wrong. The officers in the room will do their write-ups and from the initial interviews you were only defending yourself."

Peter stood shook hands with the warden. He was relieved, but something in his head didn't feel right. He knew that Bonner had made a move for him, but he also knew that the man was not a trained fighter.

Was he a bully for that? And still, there were other things brewing.

On his way home, Peter suddenly felt heavy. Not physically, but his mind was heavy. Yes, Bonner had murdered his own family, but Peter thought about the things that he had done in combat.

He looked in the mirror. And for the first time in his life, he felt that he needed to ask himself if he was a killer. No, not innocent people; never the innocent. But in battle, women and children do throw themselves into the fray. So, yes, men, women, and children die in battle. But innocents?

No, no one out there is innocent.

"I *am* a killer. What makes me different than that son of a bitch?" Peter hadn't felt this way for a long time.

None of his tools were working. His mind was floating from kill to kill; he felt uncontrollable anger that gave him a feeling of fire upon his entire body. Peter drove into the driveway of their home, but he couldn't move. It would be a solid hour before he could walk in and look Holly in the face.

Holly was in their living room scanning her laptop screen and creating a lesson plan. She looked up and his face said a million words. When she met Peter, he had found a place and the tools to control his thoughts and feelings. This Peter that had walked in the door seemed to be lost and scared.

He cried as he told her that maybe he deserved to be in prison for what he had done. Soldiers train to kill, they become numb to it, it's their job. But that doesn't make it right. As a group, they never asked one another what they had done. None of it was for anyone else's consumption. The things done stay with those who did them.

Holly had told him that she understood why he

felt the way that he did, but he did what he did to survive and to come home. It was quiet for a moment, and they simply stared at one another, existing in that moment.

Peter then started, "As a trained killer, I am more dangerous than 90% of those convicts. I've killed more people than most serial killers. Why did I get awards? Medals? Why?" They locked eyes then he smiled, "It's a paradox."

Holly knew question was rhetorical. She let him speak for as long as he needed. Once he spilled it all out, he took a deep breath. He could rest the incessant voices in his head. The confusion, self-hate, and anger.

In the years to come, it would never be a thing that he could understand. It's, really, something that you never quite figured out. A soldier overseas that kills the enemy comes home to be called a hero by their Unit and Chain of Command. Sure, over the years there was push back, people that protested soldiers. But most of it was a pat on the back, a discount at some restaurants, and a thank you for your service.

On the other hand, any soldier that comes home and decides to continue killing, even if it is bad guys—well he's wrong? Peter thought it to be hypocritical.

It's literally the old, teach a man to fish thing. I was taught to kill. So, keep it going. I was good at it. In combat, Peter had mercy for no one.

Each day at his job, he walked by criminals, most of them having done less to get here than what Peter had done in his life. Sometimes he imagined being inside of a cell, locked away for his deeds. It was a thought that he kept to himself. In helping the men in group sessions, Peter found some healing for himself. It was a prisoner named Ben Willis that was sharing a memory that led him to seek help.

He began, "I had been a junkie, stealing and

hurting people that I didn't know and people that had once been special to me. I didn't feel good about what I did, but drugs were my reason for existing. Every high kept me moving forward. I lost everything. Every good thing in my life is gone. But I woke up, in my cell, one morning and I lay there and asked myself one question that changed it all. Am I still that person?" Willis paused as he stared down at his feet, "That was it, I'm not trapped in being that person forever. I choose who I am."

Everyone had thanked Willis for sharing and the session came to an end, and Peter sat still for a few minutes. He thought to himself: What difference does it make what he had done in combat? Yes, he could dwell on it and let it be his identity for the rest of his life or he could choose who he wanted to be. Yes, Willis, a junkie who had no real education and had hurt everyone in his life, had given Peter the greatest tool that he would ever place in his mental toolbox. I am who I choose to be.

More To Me Than You Can See

James Romano spent his life being a peculiar person. From the way he spoke to the way his sisters, who seemed to be able to get him to do anything that they asked of him. Yes, James was what many referred to as a pushover. The only time James did anything that might be out of character was if his sisters sent him to take care of someone that had upset them.

There he went, like a silent messenger of vengeance, to make sure the people involved didn't make the same mistake twice. For their part, his sisters said that they only wanted to toughen James up from being a pushover. Yet, they pushed him over at every opportunity. Susan and Becky were James' biggest enemies in life.

As he became older, he decided to try standing on his own. He would join the baseball team. James found it to be fun, he had a talent for the game, and the guys seemed to enjoy his company. That is, until a rumor that he had joined the team to be able to get some time with the guys in the locker room had been spread around campus. After that, baseball went downhill for him. No one on the team wanted to hang out with him. He quit, walking away from something that he really liked. He didn't know who had started the rumor, he always thought that it was his sisters. They wanted him back home with them. The girls, for their part, welcomed their brother back with open arms. They would tell him how people make things up and try to judge you over every little rumor.

"Jimmy, those guys are jerks," Susan told him after he had come home sad about quitting the team.

"Yeah, we've got some really cool things coming up in the next couple of months." Becky started in on him. "We can be the three amigos again."

"What do you say?" Susan stated as both sisters

stared at their brother for an answer.

"Sure." He was sad but looking to restart life now that there was a rumor floating around about him. How could everything have gone so bad so quickly?

It had been a very strange life for James. The times his sisters had made him their hit man, of sorts, it was never a really clear event. He would always remember what it took to walk over. But that was where it ended. When it first started, Randy Simms had punched him squarely in the face, knocking him to the ground. The girls had sent James over to put some persuasion on Randy for something he had done to them. When James landed on the ground, he wanted to cry. He could feel the tears welling up, but then something happened.

"What's wrong, Jane, you gonna' cry?" Randy stood over him.

James heard it, quickly closed his eyes. He didn't want the tears to roll down his cheeks. Then Derek laid his hand on James' shoulder and told him, "Sit this one out, kid. I got this."

Derek was a new student, a big guy, and he didn't mess around. Randy was beaten to a pulp. It was so bad that Randy was left there on the ground bloody and crying. As Derek was beating on the boy, James heard him saying, "Who's crying now, baby? Huh, who's crying?"

"Get up, James. It's over," Derek said as he walked away.

For his part, James would try to have Derek over as often as possible. They were a lot alike. Derek was strong, big, and boisterous.

James was small, weak, and quiet. But the sum of those parts, as different as they were, did not make them very different. They were like bookends. The same cartoons, books, and TV shows. Still, to James, it was their love of corny "dad" jokes that sealed their friendship.

Susan and Becky were mean people. Even for twins, they were eerily like one another. All the times that they had sent James; they never went to help him. Whether he got beat up or won a fight was up to him. The girls were uncaring of their parents, James, or anyone that might come in between the two of them.

After high school, the girls went to college for a semester or two before they found their real calling. Out of an old house near campus, the girls were running a small brothel and private poker games. It started slowly at first: they worked on their backs along with two other girls. A few months later, the poker game was added.   They needed security, and that was where David Cannon, a bar fighting tough guy, came into the picture. He brought in four other guys to have enough coverage and muscle in the house to take care of anything that might happen in the house. David was in charge of the poker game players and their conduct and safety. It all worked out well for a couple of years. The girls were getting rich and were happy. Until the night that one of the security guys stepped out of line with one of their girls.

Back at home, James was now a senior; he was not doing particularly well in school, and the rumor still persisted that he was a "meat gazer" during his time playing baseball. He wanted a way out of this life, and that when a fortuitous call from his sisters changed everything for him. They needed him to come up there for some security. James said goodbye to school and his parents that night. They asked about school. The seventeen-year-old said, "Fuck school!" and walked out of the house. He never saw them again.

He had reached out to Derek, and they rode to the rescue of the girls in the darkness of night. They spent the three-hour ride there telling "dad" jokes. That had never gotten old between the two lifelong friends. They had the best conversations. Derek had become the guy that could help him anytime he needed it.

James never thought that he brought a lot to the friendship, but Derek always told him that for being a pussy, he was a pretty awesome guy. That always prompted James to zing his buddy with, you're not a bad guy for being an ogre. And then they would laugh at one another.

The first night of being part of the security detail, they walked into a party that seemed like a scene from a Brett Easton Ellis movie. Drugs, nudity, and all types of sex acts and that was one of the sitting areas. Deeper into the house, they found the poker game. A lot of college guys spending their tuition money in hopes of breaking the bank. The girls told James and Derek what had happened a few nights before. A security guy had approached one of the girls for a freebie. She said no, and he slapped her around and tried to rape her. The noise brought David up and he got the guy out of there. The security guy was still here, and David told them that he had talked to the man. Derek stared blankly at David and turned to head upstairs.

Derek had found the man and beaten the guy within an inch of his miserable life. Derek's specialty, since they were kids, was making his victim cry and then begging for it to stop. Tonight, Derek took a pair of pliers with him. He had separated the man's septum from its original location to a less secure dangling location hovering just above his lip. The security guy was summarily fired for what he had done to the girl.

Derek then decided to go off script and beat on David. James joined in after a moment. They kicked and stomped on his head and back. All the while, they were laughing and telling corny jokes with each stomp. Being part of the team made James feel like a big man. Derek had never asked James to join in on beating anyone. James told Derek it felt like being free of worries and anger to help in beating on people.

"What the fuck is going on?" Susan walked in and saw David on the floor. "What, just wanted to have some more fun," answered James.

"He was your security guy. It's fucking ridiculous. He just talked to a guy that hurt one of your girls. Talked! He deserved this if you ask me," Derek said, wiping sweat from his brow.

"Nobody asked you, okay?" Becky spoke up. But after the initial moment of anger, she realized that Derek was right. So, the girls got an idea after seeing what had happened to David and his pervy guard.

"Do you think that we need new security? Know anyone that can take over those duties?"

The guys looked at one another—it was that "Hells yeah!" look that made them like one another even more each day.

From that next night on, new security was

on the job and there were issues that needed attention. The girls hadn't been properly paid by the security taking in the brothel payments for at least a year; Security was taking in the proper amounts but shaving off extra payments for themselves. After coming on to head security, James and Derek came to an agreement with the workers; they all found a happy place where rules would be followed. Money was up, fights were down, and the girls were happy. The guys found their own place. They slept during the day, got up for a late lunch, and worked out for a while.

Afterward, they went to work. The girls were there only two to three nights per week. They had found a young lady to take over the accounting. They had told James to get some rest, so Derek and James hired six new guys that they trusted.

On a night that was particularly busy, Derek had stepped away. James was standing watching a poker game. It was a quiet night, and James had met Melissa.

She introduced herself as Sassy. Sassy was James' age. She had raven dark hair in a pixie cut, green eyes, and she was short, had an ever-present smile, and was quiet and polite.

Sassy didn't really seek attention. James was surprised that they had caught one another's eye.

"You and Derek have this place humming." Sassy was the first to speak as they walked into the kitchen.

"Yeah, it's been a lot of fun. I haven't seen you before, you…uh, work here?" Immediately liking the girl, James was shy and didn't know how to ask her if she was a worker from upstairs.

Sassy laughed, it was cute, and then replied, "If you mean, am I a hooker, no. I was watching the game. I'm thinking of picking up poker."

James stared at her. He figured out after a moment that she was joking.

"Actually, I'm going to be serving drinks here. Susan hired me the other day."

"Thanks, yeah, my sisters don't really keep me in the loop about what's happening on the hiring side." James was taken back by her. She was truly stunning. There is love at first sight, he thought to himself, and continued to smile his goofy, puppy dog smile at the girl.

They talked for a bit, interrupted a couple times by Derek reminding James that he was still at work. James, for his part, gave his buddy a one-fingered salute and told him to scram.

"Sure thing, Romeo," Derek said as he walked away laughing.

Sassy and James would start spending as much time together as possible in the coming weeks. Working the same nights was a big help. James was in a seemingly had command of his headspace right now and it only got better over the next several months spent with Sassy.

James didn't have a lot of happiness that had followed him throughout his life, but Sassy truly was heaven sent. She understood his mood, sadness, and reluctance to spend too much time around his sisters.

Becky and Susan were still cruel to James as often as they could be, which was every time that they saw him. It was names, pinching, and slapping him around. They said that it would make him angrier for his security work. The girls were just mean to him.   At home, Derek and even Sassy had started telling him that he couldn't keep taking that from them, that he had to stop them.

When they were alone, Derek had told him that he could put a bit of a scare into them. James just needed to tell him the word "go".

James was not at that point with his sisters, not yet. He could put up with what the girls said and did. They were just wanting him to become a bit tougher.

In life, James thought to himself, *you have times where you must make business decisions about what you will do. Really, the decisions are what you are willing to do to others. Others—no matter who they might be.*

As a security guy for his sisters, things were going well. He had put a lot of money away and he didn't want to be doing this much longer. Maybe he and Sassy could leave soon, start a family somewhere far away from here. Sure, he thought that a new life would serve them both well. With the money, they could put a good down-payment on a home, he could find a job, and maybe Sassy could stay at home and raise kids one day. James had always been a big dreamer; his sisters called them "pipe dreams."

"You're so stupid, James. You'd fall in love with your hand if it would let you!" Susan had told him when he was about fourteen years old.

"Oh yeah." Becky joined in on the fun. "What's her name? Palmela Anderson!"

The girls' jokes and attitudes toward him

had not changed very much over his time working for them. James had grown closer to Sassy over the months since his initial idea to leave. So, he thought that he would talk to her tonight after he got home.

"Melissa, I want to ask you if you would like to leave here with me? We can go wherever you want. I want to spend my life with you. What do you say?"

James was quite scared, if Sassy were staring, she would have noticed his heart bugging out of his chest.

"Melissa? Wow, you called me by my real name." She laughed and she knew that he was nervous. "Relax, why would I say anything but yes?"

James was so excited, his smile was both

crooked and wide. He felt a weight lifted off his shoulders. He picked her up and spun her in a circle.

She giggled at this. He marveled at how light she was in his arms. They spent that night making plans for what lie ahead of them.

"I will make you happy, I promise," James told her.

Later that evening, since the three of them were off for the night, James and Sassy would tell Derek. And Derek smiled and seemed as excited as the two of them. They partied on into the night. Derek asked them where they were headed when they were ready to leave.

"It's up to this fine young lady," James said with a wide grin.

"I'm thinking San Francisco or Seattle,"

Sassy said with an equally wide grin.

"Well, the boss has spoken!" Derek said, and the three of them laughed. It was such a nice night. The last nice night...

The next afternoon, James and Sassy spoke and decided that there was enough money to leave. Derek was comfortable with them leaving now. Everything was really all set for the two of them.

James and Sassy headed over to see Susan and Becky. They would tell them that they had decided to leave. They would not tell them where they were going; those two bitches hated him anyway, telling them would only mean that they would look them up later, and James, specifically, didn't want to see or hear from them again. They walked into the house, and

James asked his sisters if they could speak with them in the office.

"We open in three hours, James. What do you need?" Susan spoke up.

"Just please go to the office, will you?" James sounded surer of himself than usual.

"Well, look whose nuts must have dropped." Becky stared at him. "Let's go, loser!"

"You two don't have to act like that," Sassy spoke up for the first time in this exchange. James looked ahead nervously.

The girls stopped and looked for a moment, then turned back toward the office. James looked at Sassy and mouthed two words: *Thank you.*

As James closed the door to the office behind him, Sassy would speak first. "Girls, we're out of here."

Susan, the more aggressive of the two, spoke up first. She sounded confused and angry. "Just what the hell is that supposed to mean? We?"

Again, ever confident, Sassy squeezed James' hand and spoke up for them, "James and me. We've decided to leave here. The job is great, but it's time to start a life of our own.

It was now Becky's turn to try to trample on them. "James, what the fuck is this about?"

James looked at his sisters squarely in the face and explained how he felt, and how it was time for him to be more independent. He could tell they were definitely angry and confused.

This began to bother James. The more he talked about the life he and Melissa wanted to have, that they were planning to just disappear into the wind and no longer be a bother to anyone, the more he saw their anger was boiling.

These stares had finally annoyed James to the point where he stopped talking about all the good things going on and then laid into his sisters.

"Look, I don't care if either of you like me or Melissa, or the two of us together. That doesn't amount to a drop of piss to me. But you aren't going to stare at us like that. So, we'll say goodbye and fuck the two of you."

As they got up to leave, Becky and Susan stared at one another. Not in anger, but in complete confusion.

"Jimmy, sit down." Susan was concerned, and he could hear it. This confused him and caught him off guard, as did her next words, "Jimmy, please."

The two girls behind the large desk stared at one another. Neither seemed to want to speak first, but it would be on Susan once again. She was the older of the two by three minutes, so she was the one to speak first.

"Jimmy, who is Melissa?" Susan spoke slowly to

be very clear.

James snapped back to his guarded stance, "Susan, don't be a bitch. She's been working here for the two of you for almost a year. You don't recognize her now or what?"

Becky grabbed her sister's arm, signaling to her that she would help now. "We don't have anyone here named Melissa. It's your security guys out front, and Rosie and April that are helping us to have nights off. That's it."

James was very upset now. He was trying to control it but couldn't for much longer.   "Sassy, goddammit! Sassy!"

"Jimmy, the only Sassy is you," Susan said quietly.

James felt like he had been hit on the side of the head. Dizzy and confused, what did they mean?

He looked over, and in the other chair, flashing in

and out of view, was Sassy. She seemed, to him, to look like a buzzing neon sign. On and off, on and off…

"What?" James spoke up.

"We figured that you'd just decided to like guys," said Becky. "Most nights that you were working, if you were in the main room watching the card games you asked them to call you Sassy. We just thought that you finally decided to come out after all the stuff that had happened in school."

James grew angry at the accusations, "You two started that rumor, so fuck both of you! I'm not a faggot; I've been dating Sassy. We're leaving here to start a family."

James was feeling even worse, making connections and feeling like a stream new data had been input and his hard drive was trying to catch up. He was muttering about Sassy, Derek, and my life… He continued repeating the word: life.

"Jimmy, please, the baseball stuff happened

because two guys saw you staring. They came to us and told us what happened. We asked them to please leave you alone, because you liked baseball. Then you quit. That's why we tried to welcome you back into being in our little club. We wanted you to feel like you still belonged." Becky said to him.   James looked again toward where his girlfriend had been sitting, he said, "No. No, no, I'm James. The two of you have always hated me, made fun of me. You know that's Sassy."

"Jimmy, you're alone." Susan sat back in her chair.

In that instant, James panicked. What was happening to him? He was alone, it all felt black. Noting added up right now, he was completely alone on this side of desk. A flood of emotions fell over him. Had he been alone every time he and Sassy spent time together? And why had no one told him before?

A spiral of memories was falling off of the

shelves that were his life. He suddenly had a very big headache. James had never had anything like that happen before. He placed hands over his eyes, he didn't want to see his sisters, he couldn't look up. He wanted to cut out all the noise that was blaring inside of his head and the sad, angry thoughts.

In the end, it did feel like he was waking up in a different world. A weight h a d b e e n lifted from within him, but things still didn't seem right.

He finally regained focus for the first time in what he thought was a few minutes, James would later find out that the few minutes were about one week later.

He was in a padded holding cell, handcuffed to a bed.

He was told that he had been there for several days and that the cuffs were for the protection of the staff as he had been quite violent. He was in protective custody, they had checked in on him each day, they finally felt that he seemed focused enough to begin speaking to them. It was at that time that he was informed of his rights. One of the officers took a tape recorder out and the entire saga began.

"Hello, this is Detective David Parrett, I'm the lead investigator into case # 473275-Bravo. James Romano has been accused of the murders of Rebecca and Susan Romano, both deceased and were 22 years old."

This was the first time he heard those words about his sisters, James felt sick to his stomach. He didn't recall anything about having killed his sisters. He may not have liked them a lot, but he would never harm them. They were his big sisters.

"What? What do you mean murders?" James spoke up for clarification.

"Mr. Romano, before you say anything else,

you've been informed of you your rights." Detective Parrett began; he needed to clarify with the young man in front of him understood what was happening. The murders had been violent and made a lot of national headlines; everything needed to be by the book. "Did you understand those rights? And do you choose to speak to me right now?"

"Yes. Tell me what happened, please," James spoke quietly.

"We wanted to ask you the same question. James, what happened last Friday afternoon at your sisters' home?"

"Sassy and I went over there—" James started but was abruptly stopped by the detective.

"Okay. Let's stop there. Sassy, who is that? We've not heard that name before. She was there with you?" Detective Parrett scribbled notes onto a yellow legal pad.

"Sorry, I meant Melissa, she was working evenings at the poker games," James speaks but is unsure of the information that he is providing.

"Okay, James, there are a few things you just brought up t h a t are concerning. First, what poker games are you talking about?" Detective Parrett sounded confused.

"My sisters were running a brothel and poker game out of house. I met Melissa there one night as I was working security."

"James, your sisters were graduate students at the university. Rebecca was studying Psychology and Susan was earning her master's degree in education. We have proof that they have both been enrolled in school for the last five years nonstop. So, where is this coming from?"

"My sisters were not in school, detective; they dropped out. Please don't tell my parents, but they started sleeping with guys for money, and their friend David started a poker game to bring in more money. After one of David's guys got out of hand with one of the girls, they called me. My friend Derek and I came and started running security. A few months later is when I met Sassy." James was trying to be as honest as possible.

Detective Parrett sat back, dropped his pen onto the pad with a quiet thud, and took a deep breath. He then thanked James for his help and honesty. The detective stepped out thoroughly, confused by what James was saying. None of it made sense, but Parrett knew that the boy believed everything that he was saying.

James lay in his bed thinking, could his sisters really be gone? It didn't make sense. He remembered he had a headache, and he'd had trouble focusing on Sassy. His sisters were fine when they left. They had left? What were they telling him?

James was all alone in his room. He was having some trouble now piecing things together. He wanted to review, but right now he felt too scattered. Being alone had never been good for him. It made him nervous. At least when his sisters were around, mean or not, they were there for him.

"The kid isn't right." Detective Parrett spoke to his partner, "He doesn't know which way is up. Poor kid."

Detective Ralph Montez was a tall and muscular man; he had loved football all his life and played in college until a knee injury turned his focus to something new. That new thing was police work. He and Parrett been partners for three years; they were not just partners, but very close friends. The type of friends who could finish one another's thoughts and sentences, and the next thought between them was clear as day.

"The world is yelling for justice, but this kid is sick."

"Yeah, he isn't playing. I don't think he knows what hell he did to his own sisters." Parrett agreed with Montez's evaluation.

The two men continued speaking, with Parrett taking notes for the tandem.

"We'll have to get him evaluated before anything moves forward. And I don't think he's going to be found capable. The kid is ten kinds of fucked up," Montez said.

The detectives got into their car and drove back to the station. Upon informing Captain Smith of the results of the Romano interview and their initial thoughts, Smith told them that he agreed. They should arrange for a psychiatric evaluation to be done as soon as possible.

"Look, I don't want any I's not dotted or T's not crossed in this investigation. Two women are dead.

They were killed very violently, and by their own brother." The captain paused, took off his reading glasses and rubbed his eyes and squeezed them shut for a moment. Then he continued, "They took him in after their parents asked them for help. Rebecca and Susan Romano did not deserve what happened to them. Their parents deserve justice. Do you two understand?"

Detective Parrett spoke up, "Yes, sir." Over the next two months, James was assigned to a court-appointed attorney. That individual would lean on the police psychiatric findings, along with the findings that his office had found. James Romano was not going to be fit to be tried for the murders of his twin sisters.

More discovery showed that James had been considered an odd kid. According to his parents, he spoke to himself a lot. He made up stories about his sisters being mean to him. The girls attempted to invite their brother to come along with them when they could. A lot of people considered him an "odd duck", and the girls would protect him from that when they could.

James attempted to play baseball while in school, but after being caught staring at some of the boys in the showers, he quit within a week or so from the incessant teasing. After his sisters graduated from high school and moved away, things got progressively worse over the next two years. The parents had requested not to be in the courtroom with James. All of their testimony was video recorded.

James' mother said, "James would sit in his room, and you would hear him talking non-stop. We didn't know…"

The mother, Mrs. Katherine Romano appeared to have been quite an attractive young woman several years gone by; it appeared that she had aged into a beautiful lady. Thin, tall, and raven-haired. She wept at the idea that her son could have done this to his own sisters.

Mr. Justin Romano, the father of the family, was just sad. He'd worked very hard over the years to provide for his wife and children. He was an accountant for a local company, a very bright and hard-working man. His money smarts had allowed his wife to stay home and raise their children. He had always told his wife to go to work only if wanted to.   "Look, by James' senior year, he'd given up. School wasn't going well; he was often made fun of for what had happened with the baseball team. Before his sisters left, he would always blame them for just about everything. He claimed that they were mean to him, talked about him, and pinched and punched him. They never did anything like that."

"Okay, Mr. Romano, how do you know that his sisters were not doing any of that to him?" The public defender asked crucial question. This, along with the doctor that had spoken with James sitting in the room, seemed to help his parents open up to the line of questioning.

"They were always out doing school functions. The girls were gone almost every school night with one event or another." At this, Justin Romano began to weep. "My girls… They were well-liked, bright, and hard-working. They had so many goals."

"Mr. Romano, it's going to be all right. Do you need a moment?"

"No, I'm fine." He cleared his throat. "James was always in his room. Constantly talking. It was disturbing, but when he went to see doctors, they would just say he had an overactive imagination, that he would grow out of it. Early in his senior year, his sisters called to check in from school. We let them know what was going on with James. He was barely functioning in school, all he did was come home and go to his room, where he sat having conversations with the walls."

Mrs. Romano chimed in here. "We told the girls that James would not be able to graduate with his class. We weren't sure if he had enough credits to ever graduate. He was a complete shadow of a person. He floated in and out of rooms in the home and only ever really sounded animated in his room when he was alone."

Detective Montez interrupted at that moment. "Did James ever explain or did either of you ever ask what was going on in his room?"

The parents looked at one another and in an almost embarrassed whisper, Mrs. Romano said, "No, we didn't want to embarrass James. Again, we had been told he was very imaginative. We thought that embarrassing him would stifle him."

"James didn't seem like a bad seed. When the girls called to check on all of us, the final solution was that maybe a change of scenery might help him. With there being no chance of graduating, we all agreed to take him out of school. He could work on a GED when he felt ready."

"That was just three months ago. How did it all go so wrong so fast?" Mrs. Romano's tears began to flow even harder.

Detective Parrett had to interrupt, stopping for just a moment to refer to his notes. "Three months? All the testimony that James gave us, he said that he had been here for a couple of years. How old is he?"

Mr. Romano was thoroughly confused by this. "Uh, James was 18 in January. He came here at the end of January of this year."

"The girls had graduated during the last summer session and started graduate school in the fall. January was the beginning of their second semester of graduate school. They felt that having James there might be healthy for him."

Detective Parrett had more questions than he could articulate. The young man didn't appear to be lying, and he seemed to be completely convinced of very many things that made no sense at all when compared to all the testimony being given by all the other witnesses.

The detectives let the Romanos leave for the day. There was a lot to uncover in this case. The biggest question was, who was James Romano?

The reports from the interviewing psychologists and psychiatrists all agreed on one thing: James Romano was severely mentally ill. It was probable that he had up to three additional distinct personalities and, additionally, he suffered from depression, borderline personality disorder, and psychotic and narcissistic tendencies.

The issues with the discoveries were that it seemed that the dangerous aspects of his personality may have belonged to some of his other personalities. The doctors had discovered that there was indeed an existing James, but there were also Sassy, Derek, and a small child called Junior.

Junior took the reins once James was in lock-up. As he sat alone for a week in the holding cell, he had not answered the jailers when they called him James. When supervised and untethered from his bed, he sat against a corner and wept, speaking gibberish like a child or toddler, asking his parents.

When he was apprehended at the home of his sisters, he was like a wild animal. The scene could not be described in words, the photographs taken of the scene had been a sad story of animalistic violence and pain.

He had not used any weapons, at least none other than his fists and feet. James had beaten his sisters to death with his bare hands. It was torturous and had gone on for quite some time. Neighbors from all sides had started calling police just after six p.m. They arrived by 6:30.

When they entered, the only yelling came from James as he was running from body to body, stomping and punching them.

They tased him after ordering him to freeze. James paid no attention to the orders from the police. One of the officers stated that they honestly believed that he could neither hear nor comprehend them.

Officer Doug Maxwell had been one of the first officers on site, per his statement, "Suspect Romano, appeared to have beaten and stomped his sisters to death. He did not comply with officer requests to either stop or freeze. He yelled, kicked, and stomped on the two bodies.

He was tased four times, and he seemed to be physically present, but no one was home inside. It was eerie and disturbing; he only stopped when he was done."

Once he was apprehended, he was transported to the local jail. Investigators swabbed him of the blood that he was covered in from head to toe. Only after sufficient evidence was gathered was James allowed to rinse off and was dressed in inmates' clothes and placed in a holding cell. That was when the quiet man, who had yet to say anything, crumbled into a corner of the cell. He wept like a small child, he could not seem to put a complete sentence together, and he was genuinely scared by his current situation. The jailers and guards did not assess this man as any type of threat. They stayed alert but were confused by what they were being told and human in front of them.

"How could that guy have killed anyone? He hasn't stopped crying for two days," Officer

Flint said to a fellow officer.

"I know. Seriously, like what the hell?" Lieutenant Rogers replied, "They said he's afraid of the dark. That guy is no killer. I've seen killers who didn't give a shit, and I've seen killers playing sick. The person in that cell could not kill anyone."

It wasn't until the third day that the weeping man had stopped crying. In the quiet, he sat bolt upright on the cement bench in the cell, and stared straight ahead with piercing, menacing eyes that just did not match the weeping man from the past two days. Officer Flint saw the look from the man in the holding cell; he'd never seen such a thing happen before. If he were asked on the stand he would have to say that this was a different person—and this person was a killer. Flint glanced once more then had to look away.

Detective Parrett arrived that day to interview the boy, but things went straight to hell in less than a minute.

"James? We need to talk to you about what happened to your sisters."

"Fuck you, pig. I don't have sister, and I got nothing else to say." This was Derek that had spoken up.

"After two days of crying, why are you being like this today?" Detective Montez started in on the man.

"I don't cry. You got me fucked up with Junior. That little kid is always crying. Why would you put a little kid in an adult jail? He's a good kid and you lock him away alone; that's fucked up, pig."

Montez and Parrett exchanged glances; they decided to step away from the room to regroup. The detectives ended their first attempt at an interrogation. James was sent to a mental facility that would better be suited to the special needs that he appeared to need. They continued each day until day seven, a full week passed until they first met James.

The police, doctors, and attorneys had done their due diligence in moving the case forward. The defense would not be guilty by reason of insanity.

The prosecution did not want to pursue a case. Nothing could be gained by putting out the details of the killings, his inability to remember much of his life, and of course the people that lived in his head. In the press and on social media, James was being called "The multiple personality murderer", "Sister Killing Psycho", "Lost in his mind headhunter", amongst other names. The Romano family was glad that it would not go beyond the preliminary interviews for them.

Leaks from within the department had let newspapers know about the weeping baby-like Junior, the tough guy Derek, and when James was around men that he found attractive he would introduce himself as Sassy. As Sassy, he was demure and soft-spoken.

As for James, strangely he was vanilla. Nothing about James made him either memorable or established him as an actual person. James just appeared to be a vessel for the others and they ran everything. When asked about parts of his life, James had never been present and had no real memories. The things he remembered were made up from what his others had told him. From what the doctors could determine, the underdeveloped personality was the real person. James had never really worked on himself.

Derek had always stepped up when James needed to be tough. Junior was a toddler that allowed James to cry or be expressive with his feelings. Sassy was James' sexuality that he couldn't bear to face;

from what James knew, liking men was a bad thing for a man. As Sassy he could like men and not feel guilty. James' intelligence was below average; yet his others, specifically Derek, seemed to be quite intelligent. The legalities around attempting to test a personality that an individual has inside of their head, well that was a completely different story.

They surmised that James had created his additional personalities to overcome feelings of inadequacy and confusion with his life. One of the doctors, Dr. David Sanderson, added that it may have started with his sisters being twins.

James would have imagined that he couldn't be just one person if his sisters were two people. That may have explained Junior; although Junior was a toddler, he was James' old personality. As his sisters played with him, he could have imagined when he was alone that he had a twin brother.

Early on, James had gotten into many fights. But when asked about what happened, he would often say he didn't know. It would be reported to his parents that he would often fight and that he could be very much a bully. The Romanos found it strange, as he was so quiet at home. He and his sisters were always playing together.

One day, though, Mrs. Romano said that Becky had asked her who Sassy was. Their mother was confused by the question and then said she didn't know.

"It's somebody James pretends to be, Becks" Susan looked away from the television for a moment, "He always says to call him Sassy when we are playing."

The Romanos never thought about what it

might mean. That and his consistent talking in his room worried them enough to take him to a doctor to be evaluated.

Again, the doctors had told them he just had an overactive imagination, and it would pass in time.

It never did. Somewhere in James' mind, he'd thought his sisters were bullying him, that he had a friend named Derek that had been his buddy since grade school, and that he had met Sassy (not just become her) at a brothel run by his sisters—a brothel that had never existed.

Time was also a thing that seemed to escape James' ability to rationalize. Hours and days sometimes seemed to pass with no apparent notice. Then again, it all seemed to fall apart when he had gone to live with his sisters who were away at college. His sisters had told their parents that James seemed to float about through the days. He seemed to be dazed, if not just flat out lost, most of the time.

They did not think anything of it; the girls knew that their brother was a bit strange. He was still the same Sassy when they hung out together and talked about men. Still, when James was alone, he would talk all evening. But that was just James.

Over the next few years, after James had been sent to a mental hospital to get help by attempting to come to grips with his personalities and gain control of his life, he eventually discovered what exactly had happened to his sisters.

James was crushed. He knew he had hurt them; over the years he was learning bit by bit. It was in a session that he asked to see photos. He wept uncontrollably at seeing the things that he had done. James asked for the doctor to give him a pen and paper.

He then wrote down one sentence, "You did that."

James was coming to understand that at no time were his sisters ever mean to him or to anyone else. Apparently, when he was Sassy (who he thought he had met at his sisters' house), they all got along.

Unlocking doors inside of his head felt a bit like he was a complete Lego set dropped from a table. James was scared; he was slowly getting to know that his best friend and his girlfriend had never existed.

As he sat alone in his room, he felt alone for the first time in his life. The other thing that he was coming to realize was that time didn't really exist correctly in his mind. He thought he was over thirty years old. He was twenty-four.

What else had he missed or just not understood about the real world? Healing from broken bones takes time, but you can eventually take off the cast and use that appendage again. You can test out the leg by running, or the arm by writing. You can see the healing. What James was told by his doctors was that healing from a fractured mind, such as he was, was not an easy task. No x-ray, MRI, or CT could show if everything in your head was fixed.

Fixed. Could James ever be fixed? He felt lucky; he did not remember doing what he had done. He had no image in his mind of inflicting the brutality upon his two sisters on that night. In looking at old videos and reading about his life, he had learned that his sisters had loved him more in his life than anyone else. The girls accepted him as he was, didn't ask him to do anything that he didn't like or change. Initially, it was a disconnect to see and hear those things. James had to get rid of the idea that they were mean to him in any way. It hit him completely one day and he wept, not as Junior, but as James. His healthcare team had told him that it was a big step.

James wept at the harm he had done to everyone around him his entire life. He would ask to visit and get to know his parents. The Romanos, for their part, still cared for their son, but they were not able to do it. They knew that they should love their only son, but they could not see past his senseless acts of violence.

James told his doctors that he wasn't hurt by that. He understood it, his parents had raised three children, and he had taken the lives of two of those children. He thought that maybe one day they would be ready, it never happened.

Over the next few years, James would lose the complete hope of ever seeing his parents. He wrote letters, they answered at first; later the letters were answered less and less. Within a couple of years, they were returned to sender. James learned that his parents could no longer take people driving by and taking pictures or stopping and staring at the house where James Romano had grown up. No forwarding information was provided. James asked about his parents; he was told by his healthcare team that a letter was sent to them asking to please relay to James to please not look for them.

Now 29 years old, James was considered ready to be released back into society. He had a regimen of daily medications. It was for everything from depression, anxiety, schizophrenia, and borderline personality disorder. It took all of those, and he would also spend his life in weekly behavioral therapy sessions and monthly medication check-ups. These consisted of him bringing in all medications to verify that he was taking the meds and being compliant with all court orders.

James was no longer on the map for what he had done. In a time when media is shoved at people 24 hours per day, the world is a fickle place, and you fall out of favor for a new crime or criminal. James was going to be able to live a nice quiet existence.

The hospital had helped him find work. He lived alone in a dorm with other released men, and his appointments kept him busy between. James was now 30. A year back in society, seven years since the last time he had lost time being with one of his other personalities, and he was happy.

For his birthday, he wanted to head out for a dinner at a local Italian restaurant. James had to get special permission to do this, but his doctor was on board right away; the doctor was excited that he wanted to move on with his life James was excited about this as well; it was an adult thing (he thought) to go out and have a nice dinner on your own. Maybe he would try wine for the first time. It would be fancy; he laughed thinking of being at a nice dinner with his pinky out, like on TV.

He was halfway through his dinner. He'd had his salad and one glass of wine. The main course was on its way out—the server had suggested lasagna. He'd had two bites and picked up his fork for a third when he stared down.

It's what a broken bleeding skull looks like. That was his thought. He blinked a few times, not knowing where that had come from. He didn't have a reference point in his head. James was not comfortable for a moment, because the lack of familiarity with the thought was foreign to him after all of these years. It scared him.

James chose not to make a big deal of what had

happened. He asked the server to please box up the remainder of his order because he did not feel well.

He got back to the dorm. It had scared him more than he had anticipated. James called his therapist and left a message with his service. He couldn't escape the thought, where had that come from? James didn't want it to be what he thought, but he knew in his heart that it was.

He went to his room, and he cried. It was like one of those film strips that you advanced one frame at a time, the ones that you wait to hear a beep to advance. In the poorer schools they played an audio cassette, and the lucky kid got to advance the film strip. The voice was monotone and the beep made a piercing sound that burned into James' head.

Susan's face was bleeding. *Beep*. The film strip advances.

Becky was reaching for him only to be stomped into the floor. *Beep.* The film strip advances.

His fists were moving fervently about as blood flew everywhere. *Beep.* The film strip advances.

Susan's face was cracked in half; there were bubbles of blood beginning to rise from where her mouth had just been releasing breath. *Beep.* The film strip advances.

The film strip would continue through the evening, and James had long since stopped crying. The shock had just become too much. He tried to leave messages with his therapist over and over.

His last message had been him pleading to receive a call back.

James left just before midnight. He was walking down the street aimlessly. He walked into a dive bar, not the type of place or environment that James found comfortable, but he wanted to disappear; he needed to disappear and regroup. He wanted to drink. He'd never been a drinker. It was a mechanism that he had heard worked. Some of the guys in the dorm shared stories of great nights when they had been drinkers. What he couldn't figure out was why the medications weren't working. They had been working, why now?

We're more than medication can handle, asshat!

It was a random thought; it came from outside of him.

Or was that inside?

"That's our booth." A large, bald, angry-looking man snarled at him.

"I think he's gonna cry, Billy!" cackled a smaller guy that was standing to his left.

Three other men were behind them, all laughing at what was unfolding before them.

James kept his head down; he didn't want to engage these men. He wanted to avoid it all. Everything.

Susan's breasts exposed; he'd bitten through them. She was still alive aware.

Beep.

"I was just leaving, gentlemen," James spoke softly.

"Gentlemen?" the little man spoke again. "We aren't gentlemen, you jerkoff!"

He had shoved a fire poker into Becky, up to the handle, through her vagina and out of her chest. This had killed her.

Beep.

"I'm sorry, I'll leave." James could not make eye contact.

"It's too late to leave now, Nancy. You're stuck buying us drinks," the one named Billy said.

He was staring into a mirror, but it wasn't him. It was a person he had known since he was a child, though. It was Derek. Derek had killed his sisters. Derek had defended him his entire life. Derek was the tough one of the two. Not James.

Beep.

Seeing that, understanding that his hands and feet had done all of that. The sheer violence then the additional weapons used; it was a bit too much for his mind to see. Derek. Derek had always told him that his sisters were out to get him.

James sat at the edge of the booth looking down at the floor. The men pushed. And pushed. Then it was a friendly voice in the distance that stopped it.

The film strip kept moving along, James was on the verge of tears. He didn't know what to do, it had to stop. But the roller coaster was taking off. Then he felt a push, and it was definitely inside.

"Sit this one out, buddy. I got this." Yeah, Derek had heard enough.

Knowing that it was happening feeling it happening, James felt like he was lying in a swimming pool. No weight, no cares just floating away.

Afterward, James was sitting, bloodied from the blood of others and his hands were sore. He heard sirens in the distance, and he looked at several of those men on the floor in various states from near death to dead.

He had one clear thought: *Thank God for good friends.*

He and Derek sat there laughing until the police arrived. They had spoken, really it was catching up. James had missed his friend, Derek said that he was sorry for having been gone for so long. They looked at the men and knew that Derek had gotten them in trouble again.

"No, you didn't, brother." James responded.

"Every time, though, every fucking time that I

show up, I hurt people. James, I need help."

"I've been getting help." James said then paused, "It didn't help."

The two old friends laughed at the play on words. No, there was nothing that would fix this. No way out, but they could help everything go faster.

As police made a perimeter, the friends decided to run.

"James, go left. I'll go right. It's been one hell of a journey."

In James' sad final thoughts, the two men hugged.

They stepped out arms up, and then made their runs, one left the other to the right, but directly toward the first responders, they were shouted at to freeze, stop, then they were shot several times.

As he was dying, James looked up as he heard familiar voices. He looked up and saw his friends—Derek, Sassy, and Junior.

Junior was crying, the usual James thought to himself. Sassy smiled sadly and told him how much that she had missed him.

Derek the tough guy spoke for the three of them, "They all shot at you, buddy. I'm the asshole but they hate you."

James laughed and blood flew out of his mouth. The police said that as the man was dying, he seemed to be squeezing his hands like he was holding something. And he was babbling like he was speaking to friends.

They held his hands as it all went dim. He wasn't sorry, he was numb. Satisfied to know he could rest. Rest and no longer hurt anyone.

James saw that his friends were crying, even tough-guy Derek, as they watched their friend die.

The film strip ends…

Beep.

A Stills Family Story:
Requiem for Humanity

Where it Started:

I was a student of Professor Ronald Stills. After years of the World Leader's League, it has recently been brought to an end. After Professor Stills was murdered by the Deaths, several of his students (me included) went to his office, trying to preserve what we could preserve. Still what follows is what we never found. The diary is how Professor Stills had seen life. In its innocence it is heartbreaking, but the underlying bravery in his words is beautiful. The diary, though, we held onto the information until it was safe for release. Following this introduction are the words of Professor Stills, as transposed from his personal diary. Professor Stills was a kind, intelligent man who found love in teaching law at the university and in his wonderful wife and son, Duncan.

As the son of WLL creator and leader, Blake Stills, Ronald had every opportunity opened to him, and he chose the study of law and democracy. As a professor, he was a leader in the "Choose to do Right" movement, which started on the West Coast, but found its end after Ronald's own father caught wind of it and the Deaths quickly found their way there. Professor Stills was a man of integrity, and truthfully never belonged in that family. Those that knew him spoke fondly of a man that led with a soft and even voice and a tone that conveyed leadership and allowing different views rather than forcing outlooks and views upon anyone.

It was written on his death mark, "For teaching and moving forward old and outdated laws and practices."

Strangely, it was Ronald's death that spurred his

students forward to begin a grassroots campaign of bringing democracy back to the world. Professor Stills had always taught others one ardent principle:

"No one person can create and control a society. We become what we choose."

In that quiet belief, Professor Stills' death changed our world in ways he never could have imagined. To those that knew him, it was sad that he would not see the world that he spurred into existence. It became a world where people could be free to be themselves and not live in constant fear that, because their opinions did not match those of the government, that one night a Death would come and pay them one last visit.

I write this living in a world where I feel free to do so, I feel free as we now exist in a society that may have found its way back from the brink of complete destruction. The man that last led the League, Duncan Stills, was dragged into the streets and killed by those that wanted to live free and feel safe in their private lives and in public.

It took groups all over the world to act in unison. The League leaders were all taken into custody, one worldwide sweep, at once. They were not allowed trials, for what they had done to the world, they were put onto their knees and executed. The irony was not lost on their families when they yelled about the murders of their family members. Their riches, homes, and power were immediately taken away. They could live their lives out in shame of what their family had done, and how they had accepted the gains from the way their family members had taken the freedoms from the world.

All were killed inside their offices. That is,

except for Duncan Stills.

No, Duncan Stills was wrapping up league business in his office. As he stepped out of his office he was apprehended and started screaming to his guards and the old "do you know who I am?".

Then, to his disappointment, he realized they did know who he was and all of his guards had been killed as the new troops marched in on his offices. He stopped screaming and tried to be manly; that was until he found out that he was being taken into the streets.

Some things about Duncan became apparent after he was placed in control. He was not a natural leader like his grandfather. And he was not a kind and helpful man like his father. Both Blake and Ronald Stills had been very intelligent men, and Duncan was so focused on becoming the world's leader, he did not work hard enough to be as intelligent as he needed and did not surround himself with the staff to help him like he needed. He surrounded himself with sycophants that told him that he was always right. And he did not care enough about people to even attempt to become a good leader. He had just become the world's boss one day; claiming that he was chosen for this and he would become the leader needed. And on that day, he was believed! But more on that later.

What is written in the following notes are the thoughts and feelings from the personal diary of Professor Ronald Stills. It is heart-wrenching, knowing what is now known, and it was both a struggle to get through the words but it encouraging in its hope that the world would find the correct course eventually.

He was a good man. In fact, Ronald Stills was in many ways a greater leader than any other member of his family that came before or after him, and this is his story as best that I can share from all of the information gathered.

"The apathy of the few will be to the detriment of the many."

—A quote from Professor Ronald Stills, taken from his personal diary

The following is true and correct. Appreciate the words and the life that was Professor Ronald Stills.

-Gerald Sumpter

My name is Ronald Stills. Yes, the son of Blake

Stills. The man that "changed the world" and, at the same time, took much of the freedoms that humans enjoyed. My father had good intentions at the beginning; at least, that is what I understand from the stories my mother shared with me as a child.

My parents met near the end of their time in college. It was in a mutual study hall when Dad walked up to my mother and introduced himself. He was never one to be shy, she had said. It was his military bravado that always shone. He feared nothing and no one. He would bulldoze the world and the people's freedoms in much the same way over the next thirty years.

I came along shortly after a hasty marriage. With dad's political aspirations, even the hint of a child born out of wedlock might cause a stir. Mom said they were really happy together. Dad, for his part, was very happy to have a male progeny to move his name forward.

On many occasions, he had explained to me that true evolution was not fish to monkey to man; it was actually the ability of man to reproduce with woman and make a creature that has never before existed. Each new human was evidence of evolution. Dad was not a religious person; he felt that if you couldn't see it or wield it over someone, then it wasn't real. It was why he chose to be powerful. That was a real god, he said many times.

As I grew older, my father often worked a lot on establishing himself as a world leader. My mother was my main influence. She was intelligent, kind, and resourceful. Anytime that my father wanted to force his type of "teachings" onto me, she would tell me to listen attentively. After he was gone, she would look me squarely in the eye and say the same thing: "Learning works many ways; it is up to you to take the good and use it. You take the bad and learn how to make it better."

Learning to make bad things better was a way of life in my home. No, he never treated my mother poorly; he actually seemed to hold her upon a pedestal, after all, this woman had borne him a son. It was me that he saw as weak and a failure.

"Look, Ronald, you aren't a bad son, but you are a momma's boy. You're a weakling; in short, a disappointment. I see you as a failed experiment. In the wild, you would be banished to die. Do you even understand how lucky you are that your mother likes you? I honestly won't have any more of you because they may be even worse than you. Do you understand me?"

My father gave me this speech in one form or another from the time I was ten until the day he died.

I did what I could to toughen up. I played sports and joined different academic clubs. I excelled and nothing changed. I finished first in my class, took an academic scholarship to a well-named university, stayed away from fraternities, and upon graduation I entered the military as a commissioned officer.

I spent five years in the military. While in Georgia, I met another soldier, and we struck up a relationship. Captain Natalie Grant came into my life like a comet. She shone brightly and seemed to care for me. After just over a year of dating, we decided to be married. When Natalie got pregnant, we both decided that it was time for both of us to get out of the military. I was an attorney in the JAG Corps at the time and decided that after the military I would get into academia. I could become a law professor; Natalie wanted to work, but she would end up staying at home with our son, Duncan.

I remember when I was a child, my father would have meetings with the other leaders. He had many progressive ideas then. I'll admit, at first, he had a good idea and a clear vision of a new world.

"We must change everything; the world is upside down and going backward. Somehow, business runs policy and politics. Politicians might also have *For Sale* signs nailed above their doors. That must stop!"   To this, there had been cheers. My father always had a way of working a crowd of people; they followed his words and cheered him on no matter what he said. From his time in local government, my mother had been proud of how it all started for him. As my father's power grew, my mother and I found ourselves on many stages and podiums. The world loved to see little Ronnie Stills waving and then saluting his father at each event.

Sometimes, he would hold my shoulders and smile. At that time, I believed that he loved me.

"Little Ronnie Stills." I hadn't thought of that in so many years. But that was what the world knew of me. First as a toddler, then as a boy. By the time I was a teenager, my father ran the world. And in all that time, I learned that what starts good can go bad so very quickly.

"Ronnie, my son, you are the best of your father and me. I will love you for eternity."

That was my mother, my biggest fan. Since my father had so much power, I was home schooled for most of my life. High school changed that, as I was then able to attend school. My father said that the real school experience would toughen me up. I enjoyed the freedom that it allowed.

My mother died from cancer when I was in my thirties. She spent her life attempting to shield me from what my father became. He went from leader to dictator and he owned the world. My mother continued to smile on stages across the world and stayed by his side until her health no longer allowed. It bothered me that after she passed, he made a big deal of spending so much time with her and how she wanted him to push ahead after her passing.

After my mother passed away, Dad went full-bore into the World Leaders League and the business of moving their agenda forward. By this time, the Deaths Program had started. Just a few short years after my father wanted to change the world for the better, he urged the legalized murders of criminals, in direct contrast to the belief that due process was something allowed by law to everyone.

My dad told me the story of the first time that the League had come into his mind. How he wanted so much better for the world. The world would be built on merit, money would no longer equal power, and war would be a thing of the past. And within ten years, he took all of the good intentions and results enacted by WLL and flushed them down the toilet.

No, he didn't sell out for money; for my father, money was never a motivator. Blake Stills was a man of power! He wanted devotion, willing warriors, and tenacity. What he got were followers and devotees. Oh, the other leaders led their people very well, but all the ideas came from my father. Anything that he said to do, they did those things without questions. Dad was so damn persuasive. He could make the world move at his whim and he was never caught off guard; it was an incredible superpower that he possessed. In all the years of my upbringing, I never saw or heard my dad lose an argument or get the bad end of a deal. Dad eventually said that he, in fact, did want another son. He never remarried, so it just never happened.

True, my father had hoped that he would be around more so that Mom hadn't been my main influence. But it took a lot to run the world and make everyone follow a single group of men.

I felt like a failure for many years, no matter how I attempted to please him. I was, in fact, the only deal that he had not gotten the better end of, in his life. A complete disappointment, a raw deal—that was me, Little Ronnie Stills. Still, you want to be a good man in your father's eyes. My mom was the only person that I would ever matter to. Natalie loves me and accepts me for who I am, but she's not my father. None of that matters in the end, right? All any man wants is his father's love and admiration. He wants to know that his father thinks that he is successful. Well, a lot of that changed with the birth of Duncan. Natalie would let Duncan visit my father as often as possible.

I did come home every day after class and office hours ended. I was home much more often than my dad had ever been. Natalie and I raised Duncan to be respectful, polite, and to honor human life. It was something that I found important, because by that time, the Deaths had been among us for some time.

It was an aspect of my father that came out soon after he had solidly established the League. I couldn't fathom that my father had come up with this idea.

To simply kill all criminals. There was no buffer, no quarter to choose or give a second chance. I heard that it was originally members of the military or ex-service members. I don't know the accuracy; my dad never shared any of that information with me.

About fifteen years later, I quietly started a bit of a league of my own. "Choose to do Right" was originally for my grad students and juris doctor candidates. It was a hush-hush experiment.

Attorneys at this time were for legal contracts, wills, and other types of non-legal means. What I chose to discuss with my students was what the old laws would have said about what was happening in our country at the present time; how our Constitution had been crumpled up and thrown away by the League. How the world had changed their rules to follow my father's views, he called the League was a one world solution.

At first, my students thought that I might be baiting them into being caught by a Death for attending these meetings. It was a bit of a feeling-out process on both our parts, as I needed to be sure that no one would find out about this and have it reported to my dad.

I can just imagine what would have happened. About five meetings in, we finally started really getting into the meat of what law was before all of this. How people had rights, and the ability to choose so many things about the world around them. Freedom had been taken, choice had been taken, and fear had become a tool of the powerful.

Power. That was the force, the drug, that drove the League. My dad, for what I knew, ruled with an iron fist in meetings. And he pushed the agenda, that he alone wrote, of the world becoming this utopia. My problem, and that of my students over the years, was that a utopia cannot just be the opinion of one person.

Still, that was the League's agenda moving forward. They said that all would be equal under their leadership. When all are together under their leadership, all are the same. Sounds simple, but by the end of his time with the League, my dad was on a different level of power.

I started asking Duncan to watch how much he

was around his grandfather. I never told him why, I just felt that my father had lost his way. Still, when my father passed away, Duncan took it harder than I expected. I knew that he loved his grandfather, but his mood and demeanor bottomed out for a long while. I did what I could to help him get better. He finally found his way when he decided to follow my father and work toward joining the League.

I'm proud of Duncan, I do hope that it helps him focus on moving forward with his grandfather gone. In my father's absence, I thought that new leadership would make things better, but one of the most horrible atrocities on record occurred about three years ago. The Deaths had chosen to move forward with the murders of children.

I was sickened. The world, I hope, was sickened by the children being left in the centers of towns all over the world. Some were mutilated and then hung from nooses; others were simply left hanging. All of it was to prove some sick point. But what was it? That grown-ups could kill children. That murder was now an everyday part of our lives as the Deaths did their jobs. Now kids could play at that end of the death pool? It was sick and did not make any sense; what type of individual could have come up with a plan like that? What sort of upbringing could they have had?

As for me, there was more interest in my group after the child murders (yes, that's what I call it), and I accepted those new students because they were brought in by other members. They needed to know about the freedoms afforded to others before them, the knowledge that murder was not and should not be legal and so easily accepted, and principles of what law had done to make the world better.

I feel good about where the group is right now. The things they are learning are making them more than aware and curious about making things better for everyone. These future lawyers are going to be better for this; I just know it! I've been careful to protect them and their identities. There are always eyes and ears watching and listening. One poster that I once saw bragged, "Death is watching."

I only share my thoughts with Natalie. She's a big supporter of everything that the group is doing; she was a pre-law student and just never went for the bar. I know that she would have made a great attorney.

Of the many things that I accomplished in life, the life I created with my wife and son are at the very top. Next to my mother, Natalie was as near to a hero as had ever come into my life, and the job that she had done with Duncan was amazing. He's a good man, and I'm very proud of the man that he has become. As I do every night as I finish my writings for the evening, I'll say: to be continued!

Note from Gerald Sumpter:

This writing was the next to last of Professor Stills' entries.

No Rest for the Weary:

Those were, or rather they will always be, the incomplete writings of Professor Ronald Stills. Later that night, a Death visited him at his home. His throat was sliced from ear to ear, and he bled out while sitting in his upstairs study. A few weeks later, his writings were later uncovered by an IT guy that had been sent to his office to clear out the electronics and format them. Danny Gibbons wanted to be sure that any school information was saved, and any personal information was destroyed.

The thing about Danny was that he was just as disillusioned with the system as Professor Stills was. So much so that he read a bit of it and knew that it might make a difference.

It found its way to me. My name is Gerald Sumpter. I am an archivist and WLL historian. Danny knew bringing this to me would put it in good hands. Professor Stills had been gone for almost two months when Danny finally found me.

With the Deaths hiding around every corner, it has become very difficult to know who you can trust. After the professor was killed, all the students in his hidden group scattered for safety. I looked for a while and found a few that were helpful with what they were able to share about the professor, mainly observations, anecdotes, and memories. No one would officially go on the record. Hell, I don't blame them; I didn't at first, but it had to be done.

It was all right; I got a good feel for the son of this system's architect. Ron Stills was a devoted son, husband, and father. Shaking as hard as I could, I wasn't getting anything negative to fall from this man's tree of life that didn't ring true. But you do a bit more shaking, and the trees nearby will sometimes yield some startingly bad fruit.

In reading Professor Sitlls' information, I found that his chance meeting with Natalie Grant was anything but chance. Of course, Ron had been the bane of his father's existence, so how better to make things change and keep him on the straight and narrow? Few knew much about her before she met Stills, but Natalie had been an employee of Blake Stills.

It is not known how long Natalie had been on the Stills payroll, but she was tasked with giving Blake a grandson. A new progeny, of sorts, that he could mold. This became the source of many conspiracy theories after Professor Stills' passing.

First, it was thought that Natalie had been the Death that murdered Ron. Next, that the boy (Duncan) had actually belonged to Blake (sadly, this one gained steam and at the same time was all but verified during at her execution), or even that Duncan and his mother had taken out Professor Stills together.

None of it rang true to me. It was all muddled really, it was hard to verify much of anything. The Profesor had felt loved by his wife, mother, and son. He also felt that his father saw him as a failure; it didn't take reading his words to know this.

Over the years, in any picture ever taken of the Stills family, Professor Stills was always sad. Sure, he smiled, but it was the smile of a gutted man. His face, anytime he was seen around his father, was a statement in quiet sadness, a fake smile plastered upon it. Ron had been in the public eye since he was a toddler, a prop for his father's unquenchable thirst for power. A sad fucking prop, poor kid. He only seemed happy on the public stage once he had met and married Natalie. It's a good thing that he never knew that she was sent there to spy and keep him in line for his father.

Other things that came out in the wash included that the son, Duncan, saw his grandfather much more often than Ronald would ever know. It was apparent in his diary that he thought Natalie stayed home much more than she actually did.

Duncan, the current fearless leader of the League, saw his grandfather almost daily. Natalie would bring him to see and be indoctrinated by his grandfather in an office only known to the three of them. In digging into everything available online and through some less than safe sites, Natalie Stills was planted into the same military unit as Ron by Blake Stills. She was not in pre-law or any other program as such; from the research gathered, it appears she was military counterintelligence early in her career; she disappeared for several years and resurfaced as a captain in Ron's unit.

Digging just a bit further, she became security somewhere in the League. That is presumed to be the place that she first came in contact with Blake Stills. It is only a theory, but in those few years he conditioned her and there was some endgame in it for her. After Ron was murdered, it was just her and Duncan, so she had the support of the entire League. In addition to this, after the elder Stills passed away, many of the men sitting on the League began to have a want for money; they said a big screw you to just wanting power. It was easy, with nothing and no one to stand against them.

Plus, the Deaths were weaponized against the voices that started to be heard rumbling. It appeared that the Deaths had become silencers and hitmen.

What had the League become? Money-grubbing killers with neither the skill nor backbone to do any of the killing themselves. Blake Stills was a narcissist, heavy-handed, mean, and a killer in his own right; he had started with a clear vision that had been perverted over the decades.

What Ron was never able to see was what type of man his son would become. No one could have predicted that the man would be pulled into the streets and killed in a very public and slow execution. Duncan was very much the product of the indoctrination that he received. He gave no quarter, and he was persistent and a megalomaniac. As the League leader, he took the world into further depravity.

He created a barbaric new state of existence; the Deaths no longer had to hide. Duncan brought a gladiator-like game to the public where any Death could take out a "subversive" (yes, he literally made up a name for the victims of his game) in any manner in which they chose.

After one month of those games, the underground grew louder. New voices would rise up from the ashes of the dystopia that the world had been dropped into the lap of. Word was, it started with some of the Deaths that found it to be a job and thought that weaponizing them to take out enemies of the state was very cowardly. It was a much smaller government, but they had become what Blake Stills wanted to destroy in his lifetime: money-hungry, weak-minded followers that would never have been a part of his League. They were encouraged to sink deeper into depravity and be worse each day by the corrupt man that would lead them to the end, Duncan Stills.

On the afternoon that he was dragged from his high seat, he saw his mother for the last time. They shared their final few moments together. As he screamed—a song to the many gathered there, and those that had taken the day to see him dragged out—it became all the louder when he saw the naked figure of Natalie Stills strung up by her ankles.

"Mother!" he screamed.

That one word made the crowd cheer even louder. Natalie Stills screamed for her son. No one could save her—no more Blake to hide her, and Duncan was of no use. However, she had ended up in the bed of Ron Stills, and maybe in the bed of Blake Stills, all of her power and protection were now gone.

The naked middle-aged woman was tied spread-eagle by her ankles and grounded by cords tied to her wrists being weighed down by stones. It was a sight, and cameras abounded as the League was brought to its bitter end.

Natalie met her end about three hours into the event. Duncan looked upon his mother as she was hacked in half at the waist. It took three hits from a wayward axe used by a Death. It might have been four, but the stones weighing down the wrists were heavy enough to tear her in half cleanly. Her lower half bounced up wildly as it was set free from the remainder of her.

The crowd cheered and took pictures of the flying body. But Duncan Stills screamed and wept at what had happened. He was stripped naked and made to stand on the center podium of the atrium established for the League's press conferences and photo-ops.

Now, he stood there this weak man and feeble man; he wanted to be a leader like his grandfather, but he was too much of a weasel. No matter the upbringing his grandfather had bestowed up on him with his knowledge, leadership skills, and strength in the numbers of those who would follow him. He was idealistic in words only. Maybe he had even convinced himself that he was right to lead the League.

But he brought it all to a screeching halt by caving to money interests, then being caught with a few "ladies of the night" while visiting a foreign country and made a patsy for the interests of the people that caught him with his pants down. Shameful as it was, he had opened himself up to it on his own.

It's strange, the men that could never be with those types of women always think they are handsome, that they could be with any woman, and that people like them for them. They are easily compromised because of their unabashed narcissism. Undone an unrealistic sense of being. The power with which they're raised gives them an unrealistic worldview. Many powerful men before him fell this way, ridiculous old men who bought young women that sold themselves to the highest bidder. Who looked worse: the ridiculous men, or the women that dealt themselves and slept with these men? It's really a chicken egg thing.

After standing for a few hours alone, yelled at by onlookers and weeping, mercifully, the stoning began. The stones were of all shapes and sizes. It started by hitting him in the legs, up to torso and arms.

A young man named James walked up to fallen man and told him to look up at him. A bloody Duncan Stills looked up and saw a face which had never seen.

But James had looked into those eyes before, James' father had been taken out by a Death, Duncan Stills, for writing an article for an online newspaper not approved by the League. It had been critical of the League's leadership, namely an elderly Blake Stills, now clearly in his final years.

Duncan had entered their home and killed the man. What he didn't know was that James was lying under the dining room table playing and had seen everything. Duncan had sneaked up behind the man, pulled his head back, and cut his oat open, then laughed.

James recalled the cruel words from Duncan at that moment; his father's final moments: "Fuck you, writer! You stupid piece of shit! Scream for me!!"

Duncan jerked the man's head back, making the blood spill more quickly and spew even farther. James recalled the blood hitting him in the face; he was about to scream, but saw his father look down at him.

James would never forget his father's final moments, the man's expression said it all, "Stay quiet, don't cry. I love you."

His father's dying act was looking down at his son and waving him to be quiet, stopping that scream.

The only thing that James wanted was one last request from Duncan. "Leader Stills, scream for me!"

Duncan didn't know what he meant until the man began dropping stones directly onto him. He screamed over and over until James was tired of hearing him. James walked away, took out a knife, and cut the rope that was holding one of Natalie's wrists. He took the stone over and Duncan let out one last scream as his face was crushed by the weeping man, putting a final nail into the coffin of the League.

After it ended, all the carnage of the day from the death of, Natalie and the stoning of Duncan, was all cleaned up and the sidewalks washed. In the hours proceeding, it appeared that it had never happened. The world would soon find its new path. It would be a painful journey, a journey of discovery and regaining a footing in a world that had long ago lost its way.

There is no perfection when many people can choose their own way of life. But that is a real society; there are many voices, opinions, and ways to lead. When people cannot freely express opinions, comment on leadership, or choose how they wish to live, it becomes negative for everyone except the ruling class.

An entire world cannot just be what one man thinks it should be. There is no future once that person is gone. The snake dies once the head is chopped off. All the sycophants are wastes of space when it comes to being leaders themselves. Most of them, on their own, are quite buffoonish and not intelligent enough to have held any position of authority. They would have been the leader if that wasn't the case.

As I write this, the world has started to heal and is establishing its own governments once again. It's taking time to find good leaders and re-establish a governance structure amongst the people. The Deaths are no more; they actually walked away easier than anyone could have expected.

The Deaths were all let to walk away. Unfortunately, only knowing some of them, it was hard to move forward with any sort of prosecution. It was impossible to forgive and forget, but we hope to forget it all happened.

None of the leaders from the League were left alive; maybe they all didn't deserve to die, but such is life.

The world was never meant to exist in a single dome. Every society must live as they choose. There are so many differences that must be celebrated and understood. As a historian of the world, I can definitely say that it has been a wild few decades that we hope will never dawn our society again.

Rest easy, Professor Ronald Stills. Learning from you and more about you from your words. In death, you freed us to a new beginning.

Duncan is so much like my father. It sometimes scares me. He scares if I'm honest. If I can do anything in the future, I will keep him away from all of this League stuff. Teach him that something was wrong with grandfather's way of thinking. I know that I can help Duncan. Whether we can make the world a beautiful place, as it was before? I just need time."

--Last entry in the diary of Ronald Stills.

The date indicated that it was this entry was made the night that a Death had executed him.

Some of My Favorite Quotes

"A moment spent in the company of the right stranger could change your life."

Bonus material, it was always some of my favorite stuff in a book. Enjoy, good readers…

Okay, what is this section all about? These are things, quotes, that I like to say. Sometimes to friends, very often to my son! But many of them are things that I tell myself. Life is not always easy. We can get down on ourselves when we fail to achieve the things that we want to achieve. When we wait for an answer to come in the mail, email, or over the phone, the hard part is the waiting. It seems like it can take a very long time while you wait. Then, when the answer is no… Wow! That sucks, you might think, then you try to move on to the next thing. But the older you get, moving on to the next thing becomes more and more difficult.   Your parents may no longer be around pushing you ahead. Friends may not know what you need to hear. In life, there will come a time when we stand alone and have to pick ourselves up and be self-motivated.

The quotes that follow may hopefully hold a bit motivation for you. If not, then motivate yourself! Just kidding, enjoy.

"In the face of adversity, choose to do the right thing."

"To touch the hearts of others, we must find our voice and share those words."

"Don't strive to be the next; work to be the first!"

"Making positive change shouldn't be saved for a special occasion; change positively every day."

"You can never be lost on your own path."

"When you must cope, remember:
  1. *You can handle this.*

  2. *You just have to make it through this moment.*

  3. *Focus on what you can do, not what you can't."*

"In supervision, you cannot provide motivation.
You must provide proper training to achieve the
necessary aptitude to accomplish the task at hand.
Subordinates must motivate themselves."

"Our lives are not random; they are made of our
choices. And we are in complete control of them."

"A tortured individual often tortures the ones that
love them the most."

"Standing still makes it impossible to get out of your own way."

"To teach is to enhance the future."

"Achievement is you against you. No one else should factor into your effort."

"Don't pray for health, riches, or wisdom. Instead pray for patience and endurance."

"Love is never misdirected; it may not be reciprocated or equal, but those aren't our choices. But let go when it falls into those categories."

"In looking for a relationship, when someone says no; respect their no. It's not a test, a challenge, or a dare *from this person. Respect their choice."*

"At the end of your days, will you focus on the bad? I hope not. Spend all your moments focusing on the best days, hours, minutes, seconds, and moments of each day."

"No amount of begging, exercise, prayer, or medicine will add one moment to your life; so live till you have nothing left!"

"You are always enough."

"The only failure is to not give your best effort."

"We choose our limits… quitting, failing, or succeeding are all aspects of what we are willing to endure."

In life, my thoughts and feelings have at times betrayed my best intentions. Emotion is a brutal taskmaster especially when you can't seem to control it. Whatever name you give it, any failure in my life that occurred due to me not being able to control my emotions is a scar.

These scars cover my heart and mind, and when you allow it, these scars will shut down your ability to feel new love, happiness, or sadness. Then you just exist. No one can hurt you because you aren't allowing any new people to become part of your life.

So, the solution? It sounds gross but peel the scabs. Every scab, each pull and peel will hurt. When they're gone, you'll feel lighter. You will be ready to allow the world to bring joy to you once again.

Is that all I have left to say? Not even close! Can't wait to see what the next iteration of me is going to be.

About the Author:

As an individual, Juan has had the great opportunity to be a husband and father. As an artist, Juan Alemán II has been a poet, actor, writer, and producer. He was born in McAllen, Texas, the last of three children.

After the divorce of his parents, his mother and stepfather would move the family to San Augustine, Texas. Upon graduating, he would attend college on a theater scholarship. But over four years he lost focus and direction and walked away. Away from school and a life that seemed to have no purpose or direction.

In the Spring of 1995, he joined the Army. He was in artillery, and once he arrived at his first duty station he would end up meeting some great friends and working in a fuel squad. He would serve his time state side, traveling from Georgia to Washington State and ending his military time in Central Texas at Fort Hood. Leaving the Army at the end of August 1999, Juan found a new challenge-- finding a job to support himself and his wife. And later having and raising two of the greatest children a man was ever blessed to have.

Over the years, Juan worked in television and film; he would do voiceover work and even hosted two podcasts (The 80's Hour and The Wrestling Wayback Podcast) over that time. He, initially, felt that he did not have the patience to write a story. Yet, over the years he pushed and eventually finished his first effort:

"We're All Broken", which is a children's book about not feeling that your life only has one outcome, one destination, or one goal—we need to be willing to accept change and realize the world has more to offer.

His second book, "Divergent Lives of No Consequence: Short Stories," is a much more adult take on the struggles of harsh home environments, battles with PTSD and other mental health issues, and a fear of a bleak future.

He and his wife live in Western Washington. Their adult children are making their own path now.

One last quote: *"The need to excel begins with the confidence to know that you can."*

The life that you choose should make you the person that you know is waiting to be heard, seen, and remembered by the world.

www.ingramcontent.com/pod-product-compliance
Lightning Source LLC
Chambersburg PA
CBHW060810120726
47909CB00006B/1858